FOLLOWING FRANKENSTEIN

Also by Catherine Bruton:

No Ballet Shoes in Syria

Another Twist in the Tale

FOLLOWING FRANKENSTEIN

CATHERINE
BRUTON

nosy
crow

First published in the UK in 2021 by Nosy Crow Ltd
The Crow's Nest, 14 Baden Place,
Crosby Row, London SE1 1YW

Nosy Crow and associated logos are trademarks and/or registered
trademarks of Nosy Crow Ltd

Text © Catherine Bruton, 2021
Cover and chapter opener illustrations © Thy Bui, 2021

The right of Catherine Bruton to be identified as the author of
this work has been asserted.

ISBN: 978 1 78800 844 0

A CIP catalogue record for this book is available from
the British Library

Printed and bound in Great Britain by Clays Ltd, Elcograf S.p.A.
Typeset by Tiger Media

Papers used by Nosy Crow are made from wood grown in
sustainable forests.

MIX
Paper from
responsible sources
FSC
www.fsc.org   FSC® C018072

1 3 5 7 9 10 8 6 4 2

www.nosycrow.com

Prologue

"**B**urn the letters."

Those were my aunt's dying words.

"Destroy them or they will destroy you," she said in a parched whisper as she lay on her deathbed, like a doll packed away in lace. "They will ruin you, Maggie – they have ruined your father."

I took the pile of yellowing parchment from her trembling fingers, looked into my Aunt Margaret's milky eyes and promised to do as she asked. But I knew it was an empty vow. I could burn the letters, but I could never destroy them. The story they contained was etched upon my soul – it had shaped my life so far, just as it had shaped my father's, and just as it would continue to shape the course of my destiny long after the yellowing parchments were turned to dust.

1

"Burn the letters, Maggie!" my aunt whispered again, clutching my hand with paper-thin fingers. "Promise me that the story ends here!"

I made my promise. But I knew even then that it would not be the end of the story.

Chapter 1

"It was on a dreary night in November that I beheld the accomplishment of my toils. The rain pattered dismally against the window panes, and my candle was nearly burnt out."

I paused and glanced round at the eager faces looking up at me, a rag-tag collection of dock children – the kids of sailors and sail-menders; waifs and strays and workhouse brats – perched on lobster pots and upturned barrels or crouched on the cobbles of the jetty, all listening with bated breath to the tale of the man who created a monster.

I took a deep breath and continued. "I collected the instruments of life around me, that I might infuse a spark of being into the lifeless thing that lay at my feet…"

I didn't read from a book. I didn't need to, for I had learned the tale of Victor Frankenstein before I was five years old. The story of the scientist who played God, who created a man of threads and patches, then infused the spark of life into its cold form and brought it into being. I had heard the tale from my cradle. My earliest memories were of my father telling me it as a bedtime story, breathlessly recounting how the scientist, so horrified when he saw what he had done, ran off into the night, abandoning the monster he had made. I was rocked to sleep with tales of the creature's misery, then its rage, and finally its murderous revenge. A fine tale to tell to a child!

"Go on, Maggie! What 'appened then?" demanded Tommy Tucker, the harbourmaster's boy, whose regular beatings were etched like a map of the world on his skinny frame.

"Yeah, tell us 'bout when the monster wakes up! I like that bit best!" That was Jenny Stocking, who washed pots in The Leaky Galleon and told fortunes in tea leaves for a penny a go.

I leaned forward and assumed my most sombre expression as I continued. "I saw the dull yellow eye of the creature open…"

A fine tale indeed. But a true one, for all that. My father had met Frankenstein's creation long ago, when as a young captain he had encountered the scientist during a voyage to the Arctic. Frankenstein had been pursuing the creature across the tundra, bent on destroying the monster that he had created. The unholy story told to my father by Victor Frankenstein on his deathbed would go on to shape the course not only of my father's life, but of my own too.

"His yellow skin scarcely covered the muscles and arteries beneath," I went on in my best tale-telling voice. "His watery eyes seemed almost of the same colour as the dun-white sockets in which they were set…"

I felt a collective shudder run through the rag-tag audience listening to the tale, and in my pocket I felt a familiar wriggle as my small pet mouse, Victor, alert to the collective excitement, peeked his nose into the air to see what was going on.

"I likes it best when the monster starts a-killing folks," said the little girl who sold matches on the corner of Basin Street and Pudding Lane. She was a bundle of bones, dark shadows under her eyes, and she had heard me tell the story so often that I would see her muttering bits under her breath. She knew the words as well as I.

"When the monster kills the beautiful lady – that's the finest bit of all!" added Tommy Tucker. "I wonder if 'e drinks 'er blood. Does 'e drink 'er blood, Maggie?"

"Don't be daft, Tommy Tucker. The monster ain't no vampire!" Jenny Stocking retorted, flicking Tommy with the dishcloth she carried permanently tucked up her sleeve.

"Well, 'e might not be a bloodsucker, but 'e's a right bad'un," said Tommy. "Killin' the little boy an' blamin' it on that poor Nanny. Then 'e murders Frankenstein's best friend – an' 'is wife too!"

"I think that Frankenstein is to blame!" said the little match girl, whose name nobody knew – perhaps she did not know it herself. "'E's the one wot abandoned the monster – left him 'elpless and alone to fend for hisself. No wonder 'e turned rotten."

At this my little mouse friend gave a small squeak, and I glanced at the match girl, who was staring out across the harbour where the great ships were docked, her wide eyes rimmed with dark shadows. Yes, the match girl knew something of being abandoned, I thought. She knew all about loneliness.

So did Frankenstein's creation.

And so – thanks to that same creation – did I.

Chapter 2

Sometimes I was jealous of the creature of Frankenstein. I grew up believing my father cared more for him than he did for me. And was I wrong?

My father's fateful encounter with the scientist and his creature in the Arctic sowed the seeds of an obsession that stole him from me. He abandoned all other pursuits, made voyage after voyage back to the icy wastes; expeditions that lasted for months on end, which cost him every penny he owned and far more besides, always resulting in the same heartbreak – and eventually in ruin.

My father borrowed from friends, from moneylenders, from anyone who would listen to his tales of the marvellous creation, the key to eternal life, the secret of the universe. In his pursuit of Frankenstein's monster, my dear father extended his credit, his friendships, his sanity … to breaking point.

"Thanks be that your dear mother never lived to see him brought so low," my Aunt Margaret said after friends and family had disowned him; after he had lost his fortune and his reputation; after we sank down in the world. I have early memories of an elegant townhouse in Grosvenor Square, with a carriage and a line of footmen. But by the time I was six years old we had lost the house and moved to Shadwell Basin in London's East End, where most of my life had been spent in a poorly furnished lodging near the docks, surrounded by the smell of fish and damp.

Not that life on the docks was all bad. I had inherited my father's restlessness and curiosity – and the Basin was full of wonders: ships from all over the world, people speaking in a thousand tongues, trading in everything from silks to scorpions' eggs. I might have fallen low in the eyes of the polite world, but I never lacked for company so long as I could spin a tale to chill the blood and thrill the soul. And if my father was absent in his endless hunt for the monster, I always had my aunt, who loved me as if I were her very own.

Until now.

"It's just you and me now, Victor."

My little mouse scrunched up his nose and blinked his tiny eyes twice before returning his attention to the crumb of cheese on my finger.

"It's down to us to look after Father," I told him, my finger running along the soft fur between his ears. "Though how we are supposed to do that, I'm sure I don't know."

It was the day of my aunt's funeral. I was wearing a black ribbon in my hair, and old Mrs Carney from next door had lent me a length of black linen to sew around the hem of my threadbare woollen dress. My hands were raw from scrubbing the house for the funeral party, my eyes red-rimmed and ringed with shadows from crying most of the night. Outside, rain fell in desolate drizzly sheets.

Victor looked up from his contemplation of the cheese, as if he knew what I was thinking. He had been my companion since I saved him from one of Ma Carney's rat traps when he was just a tiny mouseling. Now my aunt was gone, it felt as if he were the only family I had left, for she had been like a mother to me, after my own dear mama died giving birth to me.

Perhaps that is why my father was so rarely at home; why he dedicated his life to pursuing Frankenstein's

9

creation – for he believed it represented the opposite of death, the chance to hold the spark of life in your hands and resurrect the dead. I was the opposite – I had cost him the one person on earth he loved more than any other. And he could never forgive me for it.

And so it was that my dearest aunt had been in many ways both father and mother to me. After my father lost everything, she moved with us into the shabby little dwelling in Shadwell Basin and used her knowledge of herbs and healing, acquired from planning ornate flowerbeds in the walled gardens of Grosvenor Square, to provide comfort to those too poor to afford medicines or a surgeon.

I helped my aunt grow her herbs and prepare tinctures, and she taught me to read by poring over my father's letters. His tales of Arctic adventures filled me with wanderlust, on the trail of elusive creatures, voyaging towards the Northern Lights, enduring frostbite and snow-blindness, polar bears and vicious wolves, travelling by sled, tugged by huskies, following giant footprints in the ice that went nowhere – visions of monsters in the snow that led only to icy tundras, crevasses … and finally to ruin.

And now my aunt was gone. And my father's last voyage had cost him his ship, the last of his fortune, two fingers on his left hand and the last shreds of his sanity. He was a ruined man. And he felt further away from me than ever.

"We need to find a new project for him or he will go away again," I told my tiny mouse companion, who had crept up my sleeve on to my shoulder, where he liked to perch to get a view of the world. "We need to make him forget about this quest. Keep him here in London, make him happy again…"

I ran a finger over Victor's ears, but his eyes remained questioning.

"There's no need to look at me like that!" I said. "There must be something – some way to bring him back to us."

But Victor just twitched his nose. I could see my own face reflected in his bright little eyes, two miniature portraits gazing back at me. Neither of them looked convinced.

Chapter 3

We buried my aunt in the parish cemetery. A surprisingly large gathering attended the funeral in the little sailors' chapel down by the docks. There were so many to whom she had brought comfort – often at no charge – with her healing arts. Sailors' wives and washerwomen, chandlers and net-menders, oyster-catchers, whalers, barmaids from the tavern, dockers and cabin boys, Tommy Tucker (whose bruises she had tended many a time after a beating), Jenny Stocking (whose arm she had set after she slipped in a pool of soap suds in the tavern kitchen) – even the little match girl.

I reached out to take my father's hand as we followed the coffin into the dockside chapel. I wanted to say,

"Look! Look how beloved she was," but he stared blankly ahead, seeing nothing.

Inside my breast pocket, Victor wriggled. I could feel his little heartbeat against mine, and it stopped the world from sliding dizzily on its axis as I recalled that my aunt was truly gone.

There was one person present at the funeral who I did not recognise. I watched him slip in at the back of the chapel, then there he was again by the graveside. After the laying-in, I saw him draw my father aside, away from the earth mound under which my aunt now rested. There was a fine rain falling, and I felt stiff and numb in the black-hemmed dress, the cold winds from the ocean freezing my tears.

"We ain't seen that fella round the docks afore, 'ave we, Maggie?" asked Tommy Tucker.

Victor had popped his head out of my pocket and was also eyeing the stranger curiously.

"Nah, I'd a remembered a swell like that," said Jenny Stocking, following the direction of my gaze. "Look at 'is fine togs!"

Jenny was right. The stranger was unquestionably of noble birth. That much was apparent in his very bearing: the lofty glance, the proud eye, the cut of his fine, inky-black suit and the shimmer of a diamond pin

13

buried within his beautifully folded neckcloth.

"I wonder who he is," I whispered to Victor, who was sniffing suspiciously.

"There's summat about him," said the little match girl with a grimace. "I don't quite like it."

She was right. I couldn't say what it was but something in the man's bearing made me give an involuntary shudder, and when he looked in my direction across the crumbling gravestones, the weeping angels overgrown with weeds and sadness, I felt a chill run through me.

Victor emitted a squeak and retreated back into my pocket. Evidently, he had no great fondness for the stranger either.

Afterwards, when the funeral cakes were all eaten and the mourners had left, my father told me who the stranger was.

"Count Florenzo," he said, his eyes shining as he spoke. He seemed elated – not like a man who had just laid his beloved younger sister to eternal rest. "He knows of Victor Frankenstein. He has read of his work in Geneva, of his groundbreaking discoveries. He believes them to be of immense value to science – to human civilisation – as I do."

My father was pacing, his tie askew, his threadbare

suit too big for him now, his left hand trembling as he spoke.

"He is a man of science," he went on – more to himself than to me, for he scarcely looked in my direction. "Some journals came into his possession, belonging to Henry Clerval. You know the name, of course – Victor Frankenstein's dearest companion. Florenzo studied these, then followed the trail that led … to me!"

I watched my father's face as he spoke – the animation, the hunger that I had seen before and which I knew led only to despair.

"He has heard of my voyages – my mission." My father turned to me now, and his face was full of newborn happiness. "Maggie, the count sought me out because he wishes to fund an expedition – to seek out and recover the creature of Frankenstein!"

My heart sank.

"He wishes to take the monster to America for scientific research at an eminent institution in New York," he went on. "He has a ship, mariners, supplies – and he wants me to lead the expedition!"

"But, Father!" The words burst out before I had a chance to think. "You promised there would be no more journeys – that you would stay here – that we could be a family."

"And so we can. So we can, Maggie!" He was almost quivering as he took me by the shoulders, full of the electric energy that would not let him be still. "I have brought you and your aunt so low, but this is my chance to give you back the life you deserve."

"I don't want any more than this!" I cried.

"The count is staking a fortune on the voyage and he has offered me a share in the profits. If the expedition is successful, we will be rich beyond our wildest dreams."

"I don't care about any of that, Father. I just want you to stay."

But he went on as if I had not spoken. "It has been my life's mission to bring Frankenstein's work to the attention of the world, so that the mysteries it contains can be revealed – perhaps the secrets of life itself, the secrets that can defy death, bring back those who are gone."

"Father, that is impossible!" I cried.

I thought of my dear mother, dead in the ground before I had given my first smile; my beloved aunt – the only true family I had ever known – even now prey for worms in the cold earth of the cemetery. Nothing could bring them back – no spark of life, no monster! It was a fiction, a dream that could lead only to misery.

"The dead are gone, Father. This monster cannot bring them back!"

"But if it could!" he cried, turning to me with a terrible gleam in his eyes. "Think how many others may be saved from grief. How many may be resurrected – how many lives blighted by death may be reclaimed. Think of the riches that will pour into our laps when we discover the secret of cheating death."

"Father – no!" I cried. "Only God can do that!" His words struck fear into my heart. The scale of his ambition was so far-reaching, so incalculable, so terrible I wondered if it might be worse than death itself.

"God and Victor Frankenstein!" said my father. "And with the help of this creature, maybe Robert Walton's name may be added to that list. Don't you see, Maggie? The creature is my destiny. When I came across the creator and his spawn it was as if the curtains of heaven opened and revealed to me what I was born to do. I must fulfil my quest, or die trying!"

I stared at him. In the pocket closest to my heart Victor was totally still, and it felt as if both our hearts had stopped beating. "But if you die, Father … what will become of me?"

My father turned and for a second he looked like a different man; perhaps the man he had been before his fateful encounter in the Arctic – the man he might be again if he could lay the dream of the monster to rest. "Maggie, my dear, when my quest is over, then I can be the father you deserve."

He took my hand and squeezed it with a sad smile. We stood together in the small parlour, surrounded by the remnants of my aunt's funeral party. The light was falling outside and the small fire in the grate was nearly extinguished.

"Father, I cannot lose you too."

"You won't, Maggie. This time … this time we will succeed. And then this will all be over."

Chapter 4

That night I dreamed of the creature of Frankenstein. I dreamed of the flowing black locks, the strange colour of its skin, the watery yellow eye opening as it awoke with a convulsive shudder. In my dream I saw it lunging towards my father – not on the ice floes but in the mountains by a lake. My father flew to meet its embrace and the two were locked in mortal combat. I watched, powerless to intervene. My mouth opened but no scream came out. Instead I heard another voice – not my own – crying, "Father, Father – no!" as both monster and my father fell.

"It is an ill omen, Father," I told him later, over breakfast. "I fear this mission will be the death of you."

But he dismissed my fears with a wave of his three-fingered hand. He would not believe in the idea of his own mortality. Robert Walton could not die as long as he was on the trail of Frankenstein's creation. I had tried to persuade him to abandon the scheme. He was not well – not yet fully recovered from the fever of the lungs that had affected him on his last Arctic voyage – and his hand was still healing; he was in no fit state to venture once more into the tundra. But all my pleas were to no avail. He had sold our last few bits of furniture – anything to raise money for the voyage.

"But you said Florenzo was financing the whole expedition!" I protested when I learned that Father had sold his sister's clothes to the highest bidders in the tavern.

"Indeed – but he has offered me a stake!" said my father. "A portion of the spoils. This will make our fortunes, Maggie."

While he was gone, I was to stay with the family of a local sail-maker with a large brood of children, where I was to perform household and childcare duties in return for my board and lodging.

"It won't be for long."

"You said that last time, Father!" I protested. "And then we didn't see you for nearly two years."

"You worry too much, my little Maggie," he said,

wrapping his arm round me and looking at me with a tenderness I saw so rarely it made my heart skip a beat.

"Can't I come with you, Father?"

A cloud crossed his face. "The call is strong, Maggie," he said. "I cannot risk you falling under its spell."

"And yet you will risk it yourself?"

He shook his head sadly, and then seemed to shake off whatever thoughts weighed on his mind, all tenderness gone from his voice as he declared, "You will do as you are told, Maggie. I will hear not another word from you on the subject."

And then he was gone, and Victor climbed up to my hand and stared dolefully in the direction of the door.

"What if he does not return?" I said.

Victor turned and rubbed his nose against my ear, something he did when he knew I was sad. The velvety softness and the flick of his whiskers made me smile.

"You're right," I said. "At least we have each other."

Chapter 5

The preparations for the voyage were swift. Count Florenzo was clearly a man of substantial means and had left no stone unturned for the speedy advancement of the mission. The ship that sailed into the harbour just a couple of days after my aunt's funeral was a Boston whaler – as impressive a vessel as any had seen in these parts for many a year, with gleaming sails and polished timber that glistened in the sunshine. It was named *Moby Dick*, and it was both beautiful and terrifying.

Florenzo had assembled a crew: mostly whalers from Nantucket, accustomed to the icy wastes; a Russian or two, with whom my father was able to converse in their thick guttural brogue; a Scotsman with one leg, one ear

and a beard of a fiery hu
belly; and a tattooed harpo
Second whose father – or s
– had been the king of an
though how such a man had
ship he did not know.

And then there was Ishmael - ... man of indeterminable age, but an ancient soul according to all who knew him. Count Florenzo told my father that Ishmael had voyaged the furthest seas in pursuit of the greatest whale ever known to man, that he knew of the dark obsession that can capture a man's soul.

And that he too had seen Frankenstein's monster.

Ishmael was perhaps the only other person alive who had seen the creature. All the men who had accompanied my father on that first fateful voyage had perished long ago – as if the sight had brought a curse upon them. Some had drowned, some taken by the plague, others by drink or other foul means. All gone. Only my father was left as witness to what happened that day. Now here was another who had seen the monster; knew it to be real.

"I 'eard that Captain Ishmael was on the *Pequod* – the ship that went after the Great White Whale," said Jenny Stocking.

cannot die," said Tommy Tucker.

he *did* die but came back to life," said Jenny, mined to better him. "That the whale got 'im, chewed 'im up an' spat 'im out again!"

"Either way, 'e's the greatest cap'n ever rode the whale road," said Tommy. "Tha's why Florenzo wants him on the voyage."

But for all their tales of Ishmael, I never saw him, for he never left the *Moby Dick*, never set foot on dry land.

Meanwhile, Florenzo and my father spent many hours in secret counsel as they planned how to bring their quarry to America. Florenzo had commissioned a special cage with reinforced iron bars; nets and traps were devised; and a harpoon the size and weight of which I had never seen before constructed to trap the monster. It horrified me, as did the strange glitter in my father's eyes when he spoke of the voyage; of the riches he would find; the fame; the power. He barely slept, barely ate, his whole being focused on the pursuit of the dream.

"You must be proud of your father, Maggie," said Florenzo one evening, after the two men had stayed up late planning their journey. "Such a noble cause."

There was still something about this man that made my flesh crawl every time his eyes fell upon me.

24

"I am always proud of my father."

At the sound of the count's voice, Victor – who had been snoozing in my pocket – awoke. I could feel his heart beating faster than usual, an echo of my own. What was it about this man that inspired such fear and loathing in us both?

Florenzo was smiling but his eyes were cold, his fingers curling and uncurling round the ivory head of his cane. "Maggie." He rolled my name around his tongue, altering its shape with his foreign vowels. "You are named after your aunt. Your father's sister. Were they close?"

"Yes, they were devoted to each other."

"Brother and sister, devoted to each other?" Florenzo's fingers continued twisting and untwisting on the cane topper. His eyes never left my face. "How touching! I had a sister once."

"Once?"

Florenzo pretended to ignore the question. His eyes left my face and surveyed the room. In my aunt's time it had been modest but not unhomely – always a fire in the grate, the smell of bread from the stove, her herbs drying on the lintel, bottles and tinctures lining every surface. Now it was bare. My father had sold everything down to our pots and pans.

25

"I know something of poverty too, Maggie," Florenzo was saying, making a slow progress around the kitchen, running his fingers along the bare surfaces. I felt Victor wriggle out of my pocket and work his way up my arm.

"My father's spending ruined his family," Florenzo went on. "He lost everything. He could no longer care for his children. He sent his son and daughter away, promised to return and claim them both but … he was unable to do so."

Florenzo stopped, and looked into my eyes. Victor had tucked himself into his favourite spot behind my ear. I could still feel him quivering.

"Isn't that a sad story, Maggie?" Florenzo's fingers reached out to touch my face.

His touch was cold and clammy, though the night was warm. I could feel his fingertips on my cheek and his eyes boring into my soul. I wanted to be sick and cry at the same time.

"He found his son, but he never recovered his little girl," said Florenzo. "Isn't that the saddest tale you have ever heard?"

I felt myself stop breathing as his fingers strayed past my chin – and in that moment Victor sank his teeth into the count's wrist.

Florenzo emitted a shout of consternation. His

hand was bleeding and his face was filled with anger. I staggered backwards, out of his reach, and Florenzo caught sight of Victor. "A mouse!" he cried. "*Mio Dio!*"

Victor had leapt on to the table and was now scuttling down the table leg on to the floor towards the refuge beneath the counterpane. Florenzo took a swipe at him but Victor was too quick. Florenzo cursed in a language I did not recognise.

"I am sorry, Count," I managed to say, trying my best not to smile. "The docks are awash with vermin."

"The sooner we leave this cursed place, the better!" said Florenzo, pulling a handkerchief from his pocket and wrapping it round his bleeding finger, his face still white with fury.

I kept my eyes from his face and focused instead on the handkerchief – a pure-white linen now stained with spots of crimson blood, and embroidered with the initials "E.L."

"Tell your father we sail on the next tide!"

And then he was gone, slamming the door behind him.

I knelt by the counterpane. "He's gone, Victor."

My little friend peeked his nose out of his hiding place and surveyed the room to confirm that the count had indeed left, before jumping back on to my hand.

"You were very brave," I said. "But I fear it will take more than a mouse bite to stop whatever Florenzo has planned for my father."

Chapter 6

There was no stopping the voyage now. Preparations had been completed with almost unholy speed, and the *Moby Dick* was supplied with all she might need for her long journey north. Even the gods of the weather seemed under Florenzo's command, for the winds and tides were favourable for a departure that had to be swift if they were to make it before the ice floes froze over and barred their way.

"They's setting off late in the year for the cold lands, as it is," explained Tommy Tucker, who claimed to be an authority. "It only takes an ill wind for the passage to freeze over and leave the ship trapped in the ice."

"What happens then?"

"They 'ope it thaws afore supplies run out, or they

'as to resort to eating each other," said Jenny Stocking.

I glanced at the little match girl, who had listened to this exchange silently. She looked thinner and more tired than ever, dark circles under her eyes and her bones sticking out of her flesh at odd angles. My aunt had often given her small parcels of food, but now there was nothing to spare. Even Victor often went hungry.

I took a small crust of bread that I had in my pocket and gave it to her. She took it with a smile. I turned away quickly, so that she would not see the tears in my eyes. For I had a plan that relied on utter secrecy, and who knew when – or if – I would see her or any of my friends again.

The voyage was to set sail at dawn and half the occupants of Shadwell Basin gathered on the dockside to see the *Moby Dick* depart. I was not among them. My father had bid me farewell the night before, making me promise not to wave the ship off, for he considered this to be ill fortune. Which was fine by me – for my plan did not involve me standing on the docks waving my father off to yet another doomed voyage, this time in the pay of a dubious nobleman. "If we can't stop father plunging into this folly," I whispered to Victor, "then we must go along with him to keep him safe."

So I had packed the few necessaries I thought I would need on an Arctic adventure, and then, while the *Moby Dick* lay in dark and midnight slumber the night before its departure, I stole out of the house with a shawl pulled tightly over my head and Victor tucked in my pocket, making my way along the quayside, keeping to the shadows to avoid being seen. Fortunately, the vessel was moored close to the jetty and so it was easy enough to scramble my way to the quarterdeck of the *Moby Dick*, from where I swiftly managed to shimmy to the starboard side and hide away in a sail locker.

I had some provisions with me – a loaf of bread, a hunk of cheese and two apples (purloined – I am ashamed to admit – from the good people who had agreed to care for me), along with a fur coat made from the pelts of some small Arctic creature sewn into patchwork patterns, which was the much-loved possession of Ma Carney. In addition, I was wearing all the clothes I owned, and I had contrived to make a little pouch to go under my vestments out of a scrap of sheepskin snatched from the local chandlery. This was for Victor, whom I feared might otherwise perish in the extreme temperatures into which our voyage would take us.

But for all my preparations, and despite growing up

surrounded by mariners and hearty sea dogs in the Basin, I had never been out on the ocean before, and I found quickly that even the motion of the moored ship made me feel queasy. I had heard sailors' tales of land folk who could not keep their ships' biscuits in their bellies once they passed the harbour wall, and I hoped sincerely I would not be one of those.

Fortunately, the nausea subsided enough for me to sleep – though my rest was fitful, cramped in my hiding place and fearful of being detected before we even set sail. As dawn came, the ship awoke and became a hub of activity. The crew spoke many languages and their foreign shouts and oaths echoed off my wooden hiding place, filling me with apprehension.

"But we can't turn back now, can we?" I whispered to Victor.

Victor, who had made his way out of his snug new pouch in which he had slept very comfortably, widened his eyes in agreement as we felt the heft of the ship casting off. "I just hope they don't make us walk the plank when they find out!"

I knew we couldn't stay hidden for long – the food I had stolen would not last more than a couple of days – but on the very first evening the lid to my hiding hole was rudely wrenched open and I heard a rough voice declare, "Why, what 'ave we 'ere?"

I looked up to see a pair of mismatched eyes regarding me from beneath white brows, in a face as rough and wrinkled as a gnarled old tree.

"A stowaway!" he declared, picking me up by the lapels and hauling me out of my cramped hiding spot – and then, as he spotted Victor scuttling up my sleeve, "Nay – two!"

"Please, sir," I begged. "Don't tell the captain."

"I *am* the captain," he said in a voice as cracked as his ancient appearance. "An' I should 'ave you flogged – or, better still, thrown overboard, you young jackanapes!"

My heart sank as Captain Ishmael himself surveyed me with eyes of ocean-depth blue. So this was the famous mariner who had sailed on the *Pequod* and survived the terrors of the Great White Whale – and who had seen my father's quarry and survived that too!

"What possessed you to join such an ill-fated voyage as this one?" the captain asked, his eyes not angry but curious. "Why, none but desperate adventurers would agree to be on this doomed crew."

"My father," I said. "I came to look after my father. I fear this mission will kill him."

Captain Ishmael surveyed me then with dawning comprehension. "You are Walton's girl," he said. "Maggie. I should 'ave known."

Ishmael had set me down upon a fishing pot.

"My father says you know of Frankenstein's creation too."

Ishmael narrowed his cloudy eyes, then sat down beside me. "I have travelled much among the peoples who dwell in the Arctic," he said, staring out to the mackerel-grey sky as he spoke, his voice a slow wheeze, like a pair of rusty bellows. "There are many tales of the creature, among the Dene and the Cree and the Inuit peoples."

I looked at him in surprise. Victor had ventured down my sleeve now and was peeping out at the captain curiously. "The Inuit of Baffin Island talk of a creature to whom they gave safe haven. Some talk of him as one of their own; others say he took one of their own. Some speak of him as protector – others, of the curse his grief spreads over all he touches."

I felt the great rolling waves heaving beneath us. "Have you … ever seen him?"

"Once," said Ishmael with a slow nod. "I was with a party hunting walrus and there was a great blizzard. I took shelter in an Inuit village. For three days and three nights the storm raged – sheets of ice and snow that could knock a man sideways."

I could see the icy tundras of my father's stories. Victor shivered and my fingers tingled with apprehension of the cold.

"A child was missing," went on the old sea captain. "He was lost in the snow, the people were grieving. And then we heard the sound – something above the wind and storm, and the little boy stumbled out of the blizzard unhurt. And we saw a figure, a giant form, glide out through the freezing skies."

"The monster?"

"Or man. I could not say. The child was too young to tell how he had found his way back to the village but he was warm, almost dry. Something had helped him—" Ishmael paused for a moment. "Or *someone*."

"So it is real – not just in my father's imagination."

Ishmael's gaze returned from the slate-grey sea to take in my layers of shabby clothing, my bitten nails and pinched face, my scrawny form and my only companion – a mouse – perched on my hand.

"Your father's mind is full of scorpions, but this is not a fiction," said Ishmael. "The creature of Frankenstein is well known in the snowlands. And they speak of another of his kind…"

"Another?" I stared at him in surprise. "A second monster?"

"Perhaps," said Ishmael. "There are rumours of a child that many fear to name or acknowledge. A child with no *atiq*."

"Atiq?"

"In English the closest word might be a soul, but it is more than that. The *atiq* contains the life force of your ancestors. This child, they say, has no forebears. No soul. No *atiq*."

"Does – does my father know of this?"

Ishmael shook his head. "Your father is in the grip of the fever," he said. "I have seen it before. I sailed with a man who killed an albatross and the guilt drove him to the brink. On the *Pequod* I was captained by a mariner who sought revenge on the Great White Whale that had taken his leg. I have seen the dark fear of an insatiable desire, and all it can cost a man, and I fear the same for your father. If he finds what he is looking for, it will not bring him the peace he desires. And yet he can have no peace until he has found it."

The boat seemed to lurch sideways, and me with it – and if my stomach hadn't been so empty the contents might surely have overspilled. Ishmael caught me and set me upright again. His gnarled hands rested on my shoulders and he looked into my eyes with a sorrowful smile.

"Never fear, young Maggie," he said. "Between you and me we will steer Captain Walton through the storm and bring him to safe harbour once more."

Chapter 7

Ishmael supplied me with suitable clothing for the journey, for as the ship headed north the temperatures had already plummeted, and I quickly became aware how little protection woollen skirts and knitted undergarments offer on an Arctic voyage. I was by necessity dressed as a ship's boy, for those were the only outfits available, but I did not mind. In truth I found the freedom from my skirts liberating; my hair was shoved up into a boy's cap and a giant old whaler's greatcoat was pulled over my breeches.

I was presented thus to my father, who stood on the deck, telescope in hand, staring out across the blank miles of the sea. If I had expected him to be angry – or, better still, pleased to see me – I was disappointed.

Perhaps he could not bear that he had bought me into harm's way, for he brushed Ishmael's words away impatiently, as he did my own explanation.

"Just keep her out of trouble," was all he said. "And out of my way."

"But, Father – I came to help you!"

"None may help me, save God or Victor Frankenstein's creation," he said, his voice as hard as flint against the crashing waves and the wheeling cries of gulls. "I told you to stay at home. It would have been better for both of us if you had heeded my words."

Thankfully, Captain Ishmael told me that I must work to earn my keep on board the *Moby Dick*, for to be idle would surely have plunged me into an abyss as deep as my father's. As the ship made its way steadily north and temperatures dropped further, Victor slept more and more, slipping into what I supposed must be a kind of hibernation. In his warm pouch, close to my chest, I could hear his heart beat ever more slowly, and his breathing became low and shallow. I missed his company sorely, occasionally waking him to feed on scraps of ship's biscuit and salt pork, which were the main constituents of our mariner's diet. Otherwise I let him sleep on.

Northward we sailed, through leaden seas beneath white skies, giant sea birds circling above. Sometimes the mists descended and we could see no further than the reach of our own hands; sometimes ice floes and giant bergs floated out of the veil of white; and sometimes giant sea creatures could be seen circling in the murk. And yet sometimes the skies were clear and the sea seemed to roll to a horizon that sparkled like the end of the world. Once, we caught sight of the blow of a whale and some of the crew grew excited, calling Ishmael to pursue it with the harpoon. These whalers from Nantucket told me tales of chasing the giant beasts on the ice floes. The man called Queequeg the Second, whose father had sailed with Ishmael on the voyage to catch the Great White Whale, said many a ship had been upturned in the struggle, with many a mariner thrown into the icy floe. The Scotsman with the giant beard spoke of dragging a half-dead creature mile after mile till it eventually succumbed, whereupon the mariners must bring it aboard piece by piece before the sharks took it. Their stories sickened and fascinated me in equal measure.

As we sailed further north still, an albatross began to follow our ship, which Ishmael told me was a sign of prosperity for our voyage. It looked like some ancient species from the time when dragons roamed the earth. And now white flakes fell from the frozen skies, and the whole ship seemed like an object from a snow globe that I recalled from the nursery in Grosvenor Square. Ice clung to the sails and it looked like cobwebs – as if we were aboard a toy ship collecting spiders' webs in an attic.

Only this was no toy and the voyage no game. Indeed, I worked harder than I had ever done in my life – and in the harshest conditions too. I was not treated cruelly, but as cabin boy I was expected to scrub decks, scramble up the rigging, clean out the bilges and run any errand a mariner took into his head. I slept in a moth-eaten hammock and sometimes I felt as if I were awoken before I had even gone to sleep. The food rations were barely enough to keep body and soul together; the biscuits full of weevils; the salt beef so tough and dry I could barely swallow it. And yet, in truth, I was not unhappy. I enjoyed the work, and loved the sense of adventure after years of staring out from the Basin and wondering what lay beyond. I enjoyed the ever-changing seascape and the company of my fellow mariners. Had I not been anxious for my father – who barely left his cabin and seemed more pained than pleased to see me – I would have been as

41

happy as I had known in my thirteen years on earth.

"A mariner's life suits me a little better than it does you, my friend," I whispered to Victor as he blinkingly nibbled on a piece of salt fish I had roused him to consume, his eyes sleepy and his cold nose wrinkled in disgust. "I promise to make it up to you when all this is over! Perhaps we'll travel somewhere warm!"

Things certainly didn't get any warmer as we neared the Arctic Circle and temperatures continued to plunge, the sea taking on a new hue, a new sound, a new smell. Even the water moved differently, and the salt in the air now mingled with another deeper, more ancient aroma that seemed to hark back to the very beginning of time; of a world of ice and snow. At night we saw strange multicoloured lights in the sky – these were the Northern Lights, Ishmael told me. The Inuit called them aurora and said they were flashes from heaven – for at the pole, they said, the earth touched the sky and held hands with God himself.

By now I had ensured my place as a valued member of the crew. I learned to scrub the quarterdeck till it shone and climb the rigging faster than any of my elders. I could help the ship's cook make sea biscuits, and assist Captain Ishmael in reading the map and setting the coordinates on the compass. Sometimes he even let me take charge of the wheel; a great honour, for Ishmael trusted very few with that role.

My fellow sailors had taken me to their hearts, but they remained wary of my father, lowering their eyes when he passed and sometimes crossing themselves, as if to ward off a curse he carried in his heavy heart.

"They have heard tales of his previous voyages," Ishmael told me. "Of strange deaths and misadventure, of whole crews perishing in mysterious circumstances."

I glanced over to where my father stood at the helm of the ship, motionless, staring out into the icy mists, as if his eyes might bore a hole in the fog and reveal the creature within.

"They talk of the curse unleashed when Victor Frankenstein abandoned the monster he created," said Ishmael. "They believe your father carries it like an ill omen in his soul."

"Why did they agree to sail with him then?"

"They are mariners," said Ishmael. "Superstitious and fearful men who know the darkest depths of the globe and the evil that swills beneath the waves. But they are whalers, and they would never run from fear. And nor would you, young Maggie. Nor would you."

Chapter 8

One morning I awoke to another new smell in the air. When I went on deck, I saw giant ice mountains towering on either side of the ship. Enormous walruses and seals with their dog-like faces were following our progress as we made our way up the narrow strait. The wind was biting and I pulled forward the furs Ishmael had given me, so that just my eyes were visible, and still I could feel my lashes freezing. Queequeg the Second told me that we were in the Baffin Strait, heading not towards the Russian tundra where my father had seen the beast, but for the Canadian Arctic Archipelago where Ishmael believed the creature now resided.

Just then there was a cry from deck, and up ahead was the first human settlement I had eyed for weeks

– a collection of wooden buildings clustered around a small harbour. After so many days at sea, it made me dizzy to look at land – as if the world had been turned upside down and the rolling of the waves was solid and the mountains were so many oceans. The aroma that rose in the air as we sailed closer reminded me of Shadwell Basin and the smell of human habitation – woodsmoke, salt fish, timber, resin, the tang of whale oil – but something else too; something I couldn't put my finger on, a scent that made Victor stir in the depth of his slumber as if he were having a bad dream.

"This is Pangnirtung," Ishmael told me. "Or some call it Pannirtuuq – the place of bull caribou. These lands have been settled for centuries by the Inuit, but now this place is owned by the Hudson's Bay Company, who use it as a trading outpost."

Sailing closer, I could see that the buildings looked rough and uncared for, and the whole settlement carried an air of infinite sadness.

"The Norse sailed here hundreds of years ago," Ishmael told me. "They called the local people Skraelings – and they murdered and pillaged in the name of trade. Aye, there was no love lost between the Vikings and the Inuit, and now there is very little between the local people and the fur traders, who exploit them in their own way. This is a town built on bitterness, sustained by greed and mistrust."

After so many weeks at sea I was eager to see human habitation once more, yet when I stepped off the gangplank I felt a wave of nausea come over me. The earth beneath my feet seemed to heave and roll, and I felt Victor squirm in his sleep again, sensing my unease. The few buildings scattered around the docks were ill-kempt – a store, a tavern, an administrative office, the harbourmaster's dwelling, a chandlery and shipwright's, plus several dilapidated warehouses for storing whale blubber and furs and other items of trade. The air stank of rotten fish, dead carcasses and whale oil, mixed with a deeper stench of the drying furs that hung in the frozen air.

Pangnirtung was inhabited mainly by Hudson's Bay men – rough-looking fur traders with long beards, beaver hats and wolfish looks in their eyes. I had been eager to encounter the Inuit, a people of whom Ishmael had spoken with such enthusiasm, but those that I saw did not seem to match the captain's description of a noble people who survived in the snowlands by the strength of their wits and the warmth of their souls. All those we encountered by the harbourside seemed sullen, hostile or sunk in apathy and listlessness. I swallowed down my disappointment.

My father, on the other hand, seemed transformed by our arrival – shivering with an anticipation that appeared feverish, and keen to get moving as soon as possible. Our crew was desperate for ale and fresh meat, and I was longing for a proper bed and a wash – for I was quite certain that I smelled most peculiar. I was also desperate to taste food that had not been pickled or salted or overrun with weevils, but my father would bide no delay – we must immediately begin our pursuit into the snowlands, and if I wished to join the expedition, I must forgo all other comforts and be ready to leave at once.

So we left the crew by the dockside and went in search of transport. Ishmael spoke the local language and quickly procured a sled and a pack of dogs, along with an Inuit guide to take us into the icelands beyond the settlement. We piled the sled with hurried provisions and then, before my feet had become accustomed to solid land, we were on the back of a sled and taking off across the snow.

Victor seemed to have settled back to sleep but I wondered if he could feel my racing heart as we took off. Did he dream of flying across a carpet of white as though we were skimming through the clouds of heaven on a winged chariot? Could he hear the mournful sound of the wind as it curved in shapes round our speeding forms; or taste the new and unfamiliar tang of snow on our lips; sense the ancient sighs of the ice? Was Victor dreaming of all this? Was I?

If the time on the ship had been like a journey into limbo, this felt like a kind of heaven. I, who had never ventured out of London all my life, barely been south of the River Thames, now found myself on the back of an Inuit sled, dragged by dogs so big they appeared to me to be the wolves of my aunt's fairy tales, rising into the rainbow-coloured lights that danced in the sky and which now enveloped us as we flew, wrapped in furs from head to toe with icicles forming like crystals on all our clothing. If I had not been so afraid of what we might encounter ahead of us, I would have been happier than I had ever known.

We drove all night, although the sun never set in the Arctic in this season so the hours seemed to roll into one, and the sights surrounding me were so beautiful that I could hardly bear to close my eyes. But I must have slept, for I felt Ishmael nudging me awake and telling me it was morning. And then I saw a village – though in truth it looked like no human habitation

I had seen before. The mariners had told me of houses made of blocks of snow – the Inuit called them *igluviga* – but it was not till I saw the white domes clustered in a circle at the base of a giant ice floe that I understood. The inhabitants of the settlement were just awakening as we approached, and immediately I sensed a different atmosphere from that of the harbour village. Here I could hear the sound of laughter, children's chatter, singing and the smell of meat roasting on open fires. Though we had driven all night and I had dozed only intermittently on the sleigh, immediately I felt wide awake.

We were welcomed into the village without the suspicion that we had encountered at Pangnirtung. These people knew Ishmael and greeted him warmly. He produced gifts – tools, cooking pots, foodstuffs from the town – and in return they gave us blankets made of a fur I had not encountered before, but which warmed in a way that nothing else had done. We were offered food – stewed caribou meat, which I devoured hungrily – while Ishmael swapped news with the people in their language, occasionally translating for us. Peals of laughter rang out across the snowy tundra and I felt more at peace than I had in many weeks. But my father sat distracted, glancing around at the white snowlands stretching on either side, searching the horizon with restless eyes.

"Come," said Ishmael after we had eaten. "There is someone I want you to meet."

He took us to the largest of the snow-houses and we crouched low to enter, before emerging in a central chamber that was spacious and surprisingly warm. Inside was a group made up mainly of old men, seated in a circle – but at the head was an ancient woman, so old her skin was wrinkled like one of the seal pups we had seen on our journey. Her eyes were as large and dark and silky as that of the pups' too.

"This is Ahnah," said Ishmael, and to my surprise the old lady looked up at my father through her dark eyes and said, "And you must be Captain Robert Walton."

She spoke English but with an unfamiliar lilt, and the way she looked at my father made me feel as if the snow globe in which I found myself had been turned upside down, setting the flakes swirling.

"How do you know my father?" I asked.

"I knew one who met him once," she said.

"Who? Who knew my father?"

The circle of men stirred a little restlessly and I realised too late that I had spoken before being invited to do so. But the old lady just smiled and said, "I did not expect *you*, child – but it is good that you have come. The eyes of a child may see what we older ones cannot."

At this, she laughed and pointed to her seal-dark eyes and suddenly I realised that they were unseeing, blind. And yet she had recognised my father.

"We have come to hear the tale you told me, Ahnah," said Ishmael. "Will you tell it again to these good people?"

There was another murmuring. This seemed to be a gathering of elders, or those most senior, for they ranged in age from middle years to Ahnah's ancient wisdom. Ishmael had told me that among the Inuit there was no such thing as a chief or leaders. "The closest word they have is *angajurqaa* – it means respected older relative."

There were more mutterings of dissent, but Ahnah raised her hand and silence fell.

"I know why you have come," she said. In my father's eyes I saw a desperate optimism that made my heart cry out towards him. "I hope that once you have heard my tale, you will turn round and return home. Leave the creature of Frankenstein alone."

My father seemed to hear only one thing. "You have seen it?"

"Many times," she said. "I knew him well – at one time."

My father's eyes filled with the strange and desperate light of hope. "Tell me!" he begged. "Tell me of the creature."

Chapter 9

Thus began the tale of Ahnah.

"At first we thought he was a *two-spirit* when he wandered into our village in the storm – for he seemed to have both human and animal *atiq*; his soul both alive and dead. The people were afraid when he first approached, and many spoke of feeling a chill run over them – a coldness of the soul. There are many strange things here in the snowlands, but he was the strangest I had ever encountered.

"We did not see him again for many months, after he brought in the child from the storm. Many thought he had returned to the realm of the spirits. It was around this time the English girl came."

"A girl?" I asked.

"She was what you might call a young lady, but not like any other European woman I have encountered. She was an explorer, come to the snowlands to learn our ways, our language. She said she wanted to make a record of the history of the Dene and the Cree and the Inuit."

I tried to imagine this intrepid young woman, this adventurer, explorer. Was that something a woman could be?

"She lived with us for many months," said Ahnah with a soft smile. "She became like one of our own. She was like a daughter to me."

"Did she have no family of her own?"

"Her father was dead, and her mother … she said her mother was the bravest woman she had ever known," said Ahnah. "Truly her mother's bravery ran through her veins, for she too knew no fear, and her heart had a capacity to love like no other."

"But the monster!" demanded my father. "What of the creature?"

"We did not see him again until he saved her from a polar bear," Ahnah went on. "She ventured too far alone on the ice and was attacked. He fought the beast in single combat, then brought the girl back to the village. He had lost a lot of blood."

"The creature saved her life, you say?" prompted Ishmael.

"Aye, the people were afraid when he approached, but when the English girl explained what had happened, they were all amazed. Her saviour was injured, and she applied balms and gave him food, for he was wasted with hunger."

The whole company was spellbound by the low intonation of her voice in the house of snow.

"He had followed the girl for many months. He had been her unseen companion throughout her journeys in the north. Though she had been unaware of his presence, he had kept her safe from many perils along the way. In her he saw a kindred spirit, one not shunned by her society, yet choosing her own path."

"How did he tell you all this?" I asked, curious at this new view of the creature as protector and guardian angel.

"Over time he had acquired our language, for he had been hovering on the edge of the village, watching over the girl. He also spoke other tongues – English as perfect as your own, Captain Walton, and German, French, Italian. This was no snow monster – he was more civilised, more humane than many men I have encountered. Many villagers shrank from him in natural antipathy – but not she.

"To her he told the story of his creator, of his abandonment, his misery. He confessed all of his evil deeds and spoke of his remorse. He admitted that since Frankenstein's death he had sought out his own demise, wandering the lonely wastes seeking only oblivion. He had willed death, but as he had not chosen the spark of life, neither could he choose to extinguish it. Death did not come, nor did relief from pain and loneliness. He had determined to keep from the world of men – and yet he had been drawn to the village like a moth to a flame. He had seen the lights of fire glowing in the snowy globes of our homes, watched the shadows of life flicker against the ice-houses, and burned with longing for companionship."

Ahnah stopped here, wracked with a cough that seemed to shake her very being. I looked round the circle of listeners. Most watched her with respect and concern, but a few shook their heads and frowned. One in particular, the youngest of those present – a man of slight build and sallow complexion, who wore a cape woven from what looked like rabbit skins – scowled angrily as the old woman resumed.

"We took him in. Made him one of our own – just as we had her. In her turn, she would not leave his side till he was healed," said Ahnah, her voice thin as paper. "We called him Kallik – it means he who was born of lightning. We trusted him, and he repaid our trust. He could kill a walrus with his bare hands, and so the hunger of that winter was abated, and yet still some feared him – although he did no harm. Until…"

The old lady sighed.

"Perhaps we show most humanity in our capacity to love," she said. "For Kallik fell in love with the girl whose life he had saved. And she loved him back."

"She loved him?" said my father.

"But he was a monster!" I said.

"You have heard the tale of Beauty and the Beast? There are versions of it in every culture – people think it is a story of love's capacity to transform. They think 'the monster' is only loveable because he is really a prince. But have you considered that he might be worthy of love just the way he was?"

There was an audible murmur round the circle. The young man with the rabbit-skin cape tapped his foot angrily. "The creature had no right to claim her love," he declared.

"No more than any of us have any claim on the love of another. We can only love and hope to be worthy of love in return," said Ahnah. "And the creature truly loved Pearl till the day she died."

"She didn't die. She was murdered! Murdered by that pair of monsters—" The young man stopped mid-speech. The snow-house seemed to hum with the weight of words unspoken.

Ahnah was once again wracked with coughs, and when I saw her lift the cloth from her mouth it was spattered with blood. She looked as though she had come out of a trance.

"We should leave you," said Ishmael.

But my father was agitated. "The creature – what happened to the creature?"

Had my father hoped she would draw back a veil and reveal what he had sought for so long? Had he believed it to be here – so close he could almost touch it?

"It fled!" said the angry young man. "Ran away like a coward."

"But where is it now?" demanded my father.

"Leave Kallik be," Ahnah managed to whisper. She looked – I thought to myself – like a seashell from which the creature has long departed, leaving only the paper-thin spirals behind. "Whether it be his fault or that of his creator, he curses those he loves and those who give him love in return."

Chapter 10

Ishmael ushered us back outside where all seemed different. The sun had shifted in the sky, and I realised that the snow was not one uniform colour – there were as many tinctures of white as there are droplets in the ocean. The pallor of the *igluviga* was different from the blankness of the landscape, and both seemed distinct from the empty page of the sky, through which giant birds wheeled like strokes from an ink pen. I wondered if one could become addicted to a landscape, for though I had been here less than a day, I already felt I would spend my life homesick for this place.

We were making our way back to our sled when the young man with the rabbit-skin cloak caught up and introduced himself as Cudrun.

"Ahnah did not tell you all," he said.

"What more is there to know?"

Cudrun drew us away from the village and spoke in a low voice. "She did not tell you *how* the monster killed Miss Dimesdale. How he killed the girl I loved!"

"You loved her?"

"Pearl – Miss Dimesdale – she had a beautiful soul and she might have come to love me – had that monster not taken her life!" Cudrun's eyes glowed as he spoke, but his voice was as cold as the snow beneath our feet, his face quivering as he went on to tell a stranger tale even than Ahnah's. For he believed the usurper had enchanted Pearl Dimesdale. He told how Pearl and the monster were married, despite the misgivings of those such as himself who feared for her life.

"She cared so little for what others thought. She said she lived by the laws of her god and her heart, not the views of men," said Cudrun angrily. "But she loved too much – too rashly. When she fell pregnant—"

"She was with child?" My father's voice cut through the frozen whiteness of the air.

"Pearl did not see the danger," said Cudrun. "Ahnah, myself, even her 'husband' – as he presumed to call himself – we all trembled as she grew and she grew."

I thought of the creature's child growing inside the

English girl. For some reason it made me think of my father – who had carried the monster within for so long.

"The baby was born," said Cudrun with a barely concealed shudder. "A strange half-breed creature – a child of threads and patches. His mother thought he was beautiful."

"She lived to see the child?"

"Pearl died within a week." Cudrun's face crumpled with anger and sorrow. "Her last words were to beg us to keep her child safe – not to make him an outcast. She cared for the creature even though it robbed her of life."

"And what about the child's father?" my father demanded.

"Grief and guilt made the monster insensible. He ran off into the wastes, abandoning his child."

"Gone?" My father's brain seemed to work slowly, as if he had been fixated on one idea so long it was hard to take in this new version of events.

"And the baby?" I asked.

"Many of us wanted it left to the wolves," said Cudrun. "It had no *atiq*. No ancestor's spirit lay within this child's soul – it was as empty as the first man ever to walk this earth. And yet Ahnah insisted on claiming it as her grandson and from then on our people were cursed – with storms and endless winters, starvation, sickness. The child grew and flourished while our people withered."

My father could still think of only one thing. "Did the monster never return?"

Cudrun shrugged. "At first it would return a few times each year, to see the child, bring furs and food. But it has been many years now. Some believe it is dead."

"Dead?" My father pronounced the dreadful syllable.

"Some say he flung himself into a crevasse, others that he put rocks in his pockets and threw himself into the ice floe; still more claim he allowed himself to be mauled by a polar bear. Whatever his fate, none have seen him for many years now."

My father's face was a painting of sorrow and grief, a mirror of the creature's desolation – filled with the same despair that had, perhaps, caused Frankenstein's creation to take its life.

And yet all I could feel was relief – and pity. "And the child?" I asked. "What happened to his child?"

Chapter 11

Cudrun had drawn us away from the prying eyes of the villagers. Glancing over my shoulder I could see children playing, running around in the snow, throwing snowballs. I tried to imagine a mini monster in their midst. Was he still here – among them?

"The monster's child grew alarmingly quickly," said Cudrun. "By the age of six he was the size of our tallest warrior. The elders of the village met and decided that it must not be allowed to bring further harm to any of our own."

"*Further* harm?" I asked.

"He killed his mother!" Cudrun's face was a picture of anger and sorrow. "Some of us argued he should be put to death before more were hurt. Ahnah begged for him to be spared. Her grandson – as she insists on calling him – now resides in a cave, some miles north of the village."

"In a cave? Alone?"

I knew something of loneliness: constantly missing my father; never quite one of the Shadwell Basin children, yet no longer belonging to the world from which I had come. Yes, I knew something of isolation. But to be banished to a cave in the icy wastes, to grow up exiled from all humankind – it was too horrible a fate to contemplate.

"Ahnah visits him when she can; she is old now and the journey is hard. But he may not come near any human dwelling – on pain of death."

I felt a shiver run through me, as cold as an icicle. I was half afraid, half sorry for the child all alone in the mountain cave. But my father's eyes were shining with an unearthly light. "You know where the child dwells?"

"Father! This poor child is not your concern."

He barely seemed to hear me. The hope that had seemed utterly extinguished just moments earlier had rekindled and now flared up more all-consuming than before.

"This is perhaps an even greater discovery!" he said. "That the monster born of lightning might create life itself is a miracle – or a perversion. Either way it is of the greatest scientific significance."

"But it's only a child," I said.

"Not just any child – a monster's child," he said. "Florenzo will never believe it! We came for one and will deliver two!"

"Two?"

"The monster will surely come," said my father. "If we can capture the child then the monster will make itself known."

"But you heard Gudrun. The monster is dead. You can get on with your life."

But I saw already that this was an impossibility. To let go of the dream was to let go of the fabric of life itself, and so it was easier for my father to live with a dream than to admit the horror of the truth. He could never give up his pursuit, even though it meant chasing shadows, ghosts; even though it took him to the very edge of the abyss.

"We must capture the monster's child," said my father, an unholy expression on his face. "We must bring back the true son and heir of Victor Frankenstein."

Deep in his pouch, against my chest, my own Victor twitched violently and emitted a squeak that gave voice to the misgivings of my heart.

65

Chapter 12

And thus our course was set. We returned with Cudrun to Pangnirtung and spent the next few days in the bleak little harbour settlement, where my father shored up a group of lawless resolutes to make up a hunting party. The dwellers in this place were mainly trappers and adventurers – some from the Hudson's Bay Company, dispatched to this blasted outpost then forgotten about; or wanted men, running from the law. All were men who had nothing to lose; nothing to believe in.

From these men my father made up the bulk of a hunting team, for the mariners on board the *Moby Dick* were reluctant to venture into the wastes in pursuit of what they called a "demon-child". Over the coming days, weapons were forged, plans were drawn up. Cudrun was to lead the party to the cave where the monster's child dwelled. The creature was known to venture out at night to hunt, he told us, capturing walruses, which he could kill with his bare hands.

"Sometimes he leaves the meat outside the village," Cudrun related, as the local blacksmith prepared manacles of Arctic iron, strong enough to contain a polar bear. "To feed his people in times of want."

"So he is capable of compassion – of empathy?" I asked.

"Every predator feeds its own kind," said Cudrun. "The sabre-tooth tiger and even the giant ice bears share the spoils of hunt with their kin. He is an animal with animal instincts, just like them."

I heard what he said and could not fault the logic, and yet the creature's actions seemed different to me somehow. They seemed more ... human. And if he fed his own kind, then surely that made him human too?

Ishmael had tried to persuade me to stay on board the *Moby Dick*, not to be part of the capture. "I have seen what a whale hunt can do to a man," he said. "It can warp his brain, leave him ever after with visions of blood and guilt. I have seen a man tortured by the killing of an albatross. This is more than either of those. You have a clean heart, a pure memory. Do not taint that, my child."

But I knew I had to go – for my father, but also for myself. This story had shaped my whole life; I needed to witness the next chapters unfold. I could not put the book down now.

The night for the hunt was set – a night barely two hours long. A full moon illuminated the sky, and as we set off into the eerie white darkness I felt as if I were on the very face of the moon itself, or in a fairy world from one of my aunt's story books – a world that existed outside the realm of human imagination. The Northern Lights mingled with the moon to cast lunar rainbows across the snow and, though my heart misgave what would happen tonight, I felt a strange sense of peace wash over me. Deep within my chest, I felt Victor's tiny heart pulsing with the same strange joy.

We made it to the rocky outcrop where Cudrun identified the location of the cave. Hidden beneath an overhanging rock formation, hung with icicles that made it seem like a giant maw, there was no sign of life within or thereabouts.

"It is a full moon – it will be hunting," said Cudrun.

So the men set the bear trap, burying the giant vice-like jaws in the snow so that they were hidden. Then we retired behind a ridge to await his return.

Maybe an hour passed. I dozed, but my sleep was filled with dreams – of monster babies, of dead bodies reanimated by a strike of lightning, of my mother standing over me, saying, "I came back, Maggie. I came back."

I was awoken by a cry, and for a second I thought it came from within my own soul, but quickly I saw the true source of the noise.

The bear trap had done its worst, the giant jaws clamped round the limb of its prey.

There, bleeding and roaring, snarling in the snow, was the monster's child.

In the full moonlight it seemed to sparkle with an unearthly light. A wild creature, clothed in furs, with long matted hair, a body criss-crossed with scars and rips and tears so that it resembled my father's map of the world – bruises for land masses, scar lines for continents, bloody wounds like spreading oceans. Its face was contorted and I could make out misshapen features: one eye drooping, some two inches lower than the other; his nose visible like a cavern above a mouth that cried in an "O" of pain.

The men rushed forward, spears aloft, and the

creature emitted another cry, this time more like a wail than a roar. I caught sight of the expression in its eyes – and it was not the anger or bitterness I expected, but instead the light of hope at the sight of fellow creatures.

Did it think, just for a second, that we had come to rescue it? That here was companionship – human warmth in the desert of snow? If so that hope was shattered in an instant, as the men surrounded it, spears aloft.

The creature was surrounded, and my father – who had been frozen in trance-like wonder – now pushed to the front of the group. He was gazing at the creature in horror and joy, like a man seeing his firstborn. The child looked up and stretched out its hand, the unnatural pallor of his skin visible even beneath the anguish. It cried out in very human pain, then whimpered. Was it possible that it said, "Father?"

It was then I saw the truth. Despite his size, the unearthly hue of his skin, the scarring that patterned his whole body – this was just a boy; just a child.

For a second I believed my father had seen it too. His eyes met those of the monster's child – and they shared a common bond. Both of them were children of the creature; both born of the fevered imagination of Victor Frankenstein; both of their lives

70

had been set on an irrevocable course by the monster and its maker – a course they now shared.

But then my father raised his hand in the pre-agreed signal, and the men sprang forward with their spears and manacles and chains and did their worst.

Chapter 13

I could not watch. They said afterwards that it took ten men to subdue "the beast". They said it fought back with all its supernatural might: biting, tearing, clawing. But I never saw any wounds on the hunting party – not a single gash or bite mark or tear. I did hear the cries of pain and anguish and desperation. I heard a roar like a wild beast – but I also heard a whimper and a cry for help, like that of a child.

Ishmael had a dart, purchased – he told me – from an apothecary in Nantucket, containing a poison so deep it could send a leviathan to sleep for a thousand hours. He used this to subdue their quarry once it was in chains. Then the men loaded the helpless creature on to a sled and then on to the ship, where a cage had been prepared for it with reinforced steel bars. The crew was taciturn as we loaded this precious cargo, their faces inscrutable as they beheld the creature, but their misgivings were visible in their eyes, screaming louder than their silence.

My father was filled with an excitement that alarmed me nearly as much as his previous despair. He seemed almost to have forgotten his plan to use the son as bait to lure its father, and instead was anxious only to deliver this prize to Florenzo in New York. Though the conditions were predicted to be dangerous, he insisted on setting sail immediately, against the advice of Ishmael.

For the first three days of our voyage we were wracked with storms that nearly overturned our vessel and caused much damage, tearing one of the mainsails and damaging the topmast. The mariners battled to keep us afloat but many were violently ill – myself included – and others injured by the calamities that beset the ship. I barely had time to think of the caged creature down in the bowels of the vessel, or even tend to the dormant Victor, as I alternated between fighting the raging storm and evacuating the contents of my stomach.

There were times when it seemed that all was lost.

I heard men calling the name of Jonah, and I recalled the Bible story of the sinner who had brought God's vengeance upon a hapless ship, and who was cast into the waves. I realised they were talking of the creature. These superstitious men believed that it was ungodly evil, not my father's reckless pride, that had led us into this storm. They called on my father to cast him into the sea, but he refused. It was not wisdom but obsession; he would rather go under with the object of his passion than carry on alive without it.

After three days the weather calmed and we were able to survey the damage. The broken topmast could be lashed back into some kind of working order and the mainsail crudely stitched together. There were many minor breakages within the ship, but against the odds, no mariner had perished, and we could limp on with our voyage, albeit slower than before. But the men still murmured about Jonah and refused to go near the cabin where the creature lay. Ishmael had tended upon it during the first day of the storm but he had fallen ill with a strange sickness, and my father had taken to his cabin once the storms passed. None was left to care for the creature but me.

It was with the utmost apprehension that I first entered the chamber where the cage had been stowed.

The stench that met my nostrils was like that of a fever ship or the slaughterhouse down on the dock, and at first I recoiled in disgust, but I put a handkerchief to my nostrils and ventured into the gloom. The space was airless, deep in the bowels of the ship. Storm water swilled about my feet and not a sliver of natural light penetrated the prison except that coming through the door. The giant cage stood in the centre, and if I expected to see a creature raging and rattling the bars, I was disappointed. The monster's child lay in a shivering heap of rags, its breath ragged, and there hung in the air a smell of sickness that I recognised from my aunt's death chamber.

I took another few steps forward. The creature did not stir. In the gloom it resembled only an overgrown boy – a child like the ones I had too often seen begging on the dockside, barely enough flesh to cover their bones. It seemed to have lost a shocking amount of weight and I perceived it had neither eaten nor drunk in several days. The manacles round its wrists and ankles had rubbed into weeping sores that bled, and it had sustained a nasty cut to its ankle that had festered untreated and now was no doubt the cause of the fever that wracked its wretched body.

My aunt had grown herbs in our small patch of

ground in the yard, and made up poultices and balms. From her I had gleaned knowledge of the powers of certain tinctures and had indeed brought some along with me, to minister to my father and any others who might require it on the journey.

I saw at once that the wound must be administered to quickly, for the redness had spread already up its leg, and I had seen children and adults fatally struck by this fever.

"Wait there," I said needlessly. "I will be back. I will help."

I returned to my chamber to gather the healing herbs and went back to the creature's cage. It was now tossing fitfully as if in the grip of fever dreams. I realised that I had not thought through the business of administering the medicine. Was the injury close enough for me to reach in and treat it? As I approached the cage, the son of the monster shifted once more, moving its leg so the infected limb was out of my touch.

"What do I do, Victor?" I whispered, but the little mouseling slumbered on, heedless to my plea.

The key to the cage hung on a hook on the wall. I barely thought. I only heard my aunt's words in my head. She had never refused to treat a soul in her life, and declared only that God had given her the healing gifts and it was not in her to judge who deserved to live or die.

I inserted the key into the lock. The sick thing emitted an anguished shiver. I felt the giant door give way and steeled myself to enter, recalling the tales of the hunting party. At that moment the ship rolled on a wave and a barrel spilled noisily across the room. The creature whimpered and a shaft of sunlight fell in that moment across its face. It illuminated the strange contortions of its features, but though it was grimy and disfigured, it appeared, more than anything, childlike; sad.

I prised open the door and tiptoed inside. The stench of fever was violent. I took a deep breath, then knelt by the creature and placed tentative fingers on the gashed ankle. At my touch it jerked away. I tried again – the response was the same. A third time I reached and now held firmly. I had to clean the wound or it would be fatal – and it was going to hurt.

I grasped the foot firmly and applied the cloth. The creature cried out – its eyes opened and fixed on me for the first time. I had expected them to be yellow – I recalled only too well Victor Frankenstein's description of the creature opening its dull yellow eye – but the monster's son had eyes of sweet chestnut, which met mine with a look of agony in their pupils. I saw in them a question: why are you hurting me? And yet I also saw a resignation. This creature had been hurt before; it was accustomed to it. But nor did it fight back and I saw that it also knew trust – it had been treated with love and kindness, too. And in my eyes it sought to know if I was friend or foe.

"I want to make you better," I said, not expecting it to understand but hoping the tone of my words would signal my intention. "Your foot is badly infected. I need to clean it or it will not heal."

The creature did not move but allowed me to continue what must have been excruciating agony. It stiffened and grimaced but did not thrash out or pull away. Gradually I relaxed into my work and to keep us both from focusing on the pain I talked on, as I often did to my mouseling Victor, with whom the conversation was similarly one-sided.

"I am sorry you have been so poorly treated," I said. "There has been a storm. All hands have been on deck saving the ship. You have been neglected. But I am here now and I can care for you."

The creature whimpered and its brown eyes – one up, one down – never left my face.

"I ought to hate you," I continued. "I often think

my father cares more for you than for any other living creature – at least, he did for your father."

At the word "father," the creature's expression changed and I felt as if it mirrored the sorrow in my own mind as I thought of my own father, locked in his cabin, caught in the realm of impossible dreams.

"You did not choose your father any more than I chose mine," I said, the wound now nearly clean. "And you must be frightened, not knowing where we are going."

"Frightened."

The word had come from the boy's mouth, two perfectly formed syllables. I stared at him in astonishment.

"You … understand?"

"Un-der-stand," said the boy-creature. His voice was cracked and dry, the words clearly painful to pronounce.

"You speak English?"

"Speak … En-glish."

Was he just copying me, like a parrot, or did he really understand?

"I am Maggie," I said. "What is your name?"

There was a pause. The boy's lips were chapped, his tongue dry, but it managed to croak. "I … do not … know."

I almost laughed out loud in wonder. This thing, this monster, this aberration, as they called him – this boy – could speak in my own tongue. And yet he did not know his own name.

"You must have a name," I said. "Everyone has a name. I suppose that Frankenstein is your family name – but you must have your own name too."

The boy tried to open his mouth to speak, but stopped, as if exhausted by the effort.

"Don't try to talk for now," I said. The wound was clean and I had the balm ready to apply. "Hold still. This will be cold and it will sting at first, but it will make you feel better. Yes?"

The boy-creature nodded. I applied the first of the salve and felt him shiver, but he let me continue.

When I had finished he said, "Thir-sty."

"Thirsty? Why, of course you are. Has no one brought you water?" I saw a bowl upset in the corner of the cage – a drinking bowl fit for a dog that had been overturned in the storm and was now bone dry.

"Here." I unhooked the drinking bottle from my belt and held it to his lips. I fed him drops like a baby and he lapped gratefully.

I had fashioned bandages out of the ripped portion of the mainsail, and now I fastened these round the boy's leg. He had many other small cuts and grazes that needed treating, and, besides, he was filthy and sorely in need of food, and a blanket, and many other things that common humanity should have supplied.

I felt, I realised, angry at my father. I could forgive his obsession, his neglect of me, of everything in pursuit of his dream. But could he truly only see this child as a prize, a specimen, a curiosity – and not a reasoning animal like himself in need of care and love and attention, or at least the bare necessaries for life? That I found hard to forgive.

The boy looked at me, and I saw the first hint of a smile quiver at his lips. "Kata," he said. "My name – I think … is Kata."

"And I am Maggie. Pleased to meet you!"

Chapter 14

Soon after, the boy, whose name might be Kata, fell back into a fitful slumber, and I hastened to gather together those things necessary for his recovery. A blanket and pillow; the tincture my aunt had always administered for a fever; soap and water; fresh clothing; a little broth, which was all he might be able to swallow; and fresh water. The mariners knew what I was doing but said nothing. Queequeg the Second raised a dark eyebrow as he saw me go back and forth from the supplies room, and the Scotsman – who was known by no other name than that – crossed himself and shook his head when I asked for broth, but he gave it to me nonetheless. I wished Ishmael were well enough to assist me, but he was too ill to be disturbed.

Over the next few days I remained in almost constant attendance upon Kata, for the fever got worse before it began to improve. It was a struggle even to make him drink – his throat was so constricted he could barely swallow. I held cold cloths to his burning brow and sang to him when he raved. In his fever he spoke in Inuktitut, peppering it sometimes with a few words of English and of another European language that I did not recognise. I often heard him say the words "Father, Pater, *Taataga*."

The rest of the crew kept their distance, still in their superstitious ignorance, fearing him as an evil omen upon the ship. I suspect they would have been as happy to see him expire of the fever, were it not for the promise of the reward for his capture that glittered like gold coins in their eyes.

My father kept to his cabin and would not see me. Had he realised – as I did, ever more clearly – that the child of the creature was no monster, but simply a boy? A very large boy, it was true, but no monster, no ungodly devil. Just a child, barely older than myself. Was it disappointment in this discovery that gripped my father? Fear that Florenzo would be displeased? Or was it something else? Did he realise in his heart that this child deserved care, not cruelty? Is that what tortured him, as it troubled me? All I knew is that in the long days of Kata's illness, my father kept to his chamber, never enquiring after his precious cargo, and visiting the sick chamber not at all.

By degrees, Kata began to recover. The sickness came to a crisis and there were several worrying hours when I feared he might not survive, but he rallied and the fever broke. And then I began to see a change in him. He drank and even ate a little, there were periods of wakefulness when he seemed to recognise me – even call me by my name – before falling back once more into unknowing slumber.

One morning I woke up to feel a lightness in the air, like the first day of spring. Victor too was stirring, wriggling in my pocket as if shuffling his way up out of the dark tunnel of sleep. I had taken to sleeping in the cage alongside Kata, and as I sat up that morning he opened his toffee-brown eyes and looked at me.

"Maggie?" he said, my name forming a question on his lips.

"Yes," I said. "It's me. I'm here. I've been here all along."

He looked around. I had cleaned out the cage and done my best to make it more comfortable for him but he did not seem to recognise his whereabouts.

84

"Where am I?"

"You are on a ship," I said.

Kata looked puzzled. In my pocket I felt Victor do a series of wiggles.

"On the sea – like, a boat. A big boat." I tried to recall the vessels I had seen the Inuit using.

"A ... boat?"

"That's why we are rocking," I tried to explain. "We are on the sea."

He still seemed confused. The long fever had disoriented him and, after all, he had known no life beyond the village and the cave.

"You were captured. They are taking you to America," I said. "New York." As he clearly did not understand I tried to tell him what I knew. "Far away. A big city. No snow. Many, many people."

"Why?" asked Kata.

It was a big question, the answer made up of a story that stretched back two generations behind him. A story of prejudice and cruelty and indifference. I did not know how to begin to tell it, so all I said was, "I suppose it's because you are different."

"Because I am ... different." It was clear to see that all of his existence so far had been shaped by this one simple truth.

Kata looked healthier now that he had washed the grime off his face and the cuts and wounds that criss-crossed his body were healing. Some colour was returning to his skin, and his bright eyes were like flowers blooming in his ravaged face. His hand reached out across the floor of the cage on which he lay and I sat, and it touched mine. It was almost twice the size of my own, the nails filthy, but it was warm to the touch, not the icy grip of a snow monster.

"So are you really called Kata?" I said.

"They say my father wanted to call me Victor."

I nearly laughed out loud and from deep within his pouch, my own Victor emitted a sound that was half yawn, half sigh.

"Ahnah sometimes called me Nukilik – which is boy who is stronger than he knows – and the people called me Tariaksuq – half man, half shadow monster." He hesitated for a moment, looked down at his grubby fingernails. "Kata was the name my mother gave me. It is short for Kataulak, which means of the rainbow – for she said my *atiq*, my soul, came from the very aurora itself. But nobody calls me it. Not since she died."

He paused and looked at me with those big, sad caramel eyes.

"But it is your name," I said.

"Yes," said the child.

"Then I will call you Kata," I said. "Rainbow boy – I like it!"

Chapter 15

That day saw a rapid improvement as the fever dropped from Kata and he was able to munch on some ship's biscuit and even sit up for a short period. I stayed with him, departing only to gather provisions and mix up a tincture that my aunt had given to those regaining strength after a fever.

Kata seemed surprised when I returned soon afterwards, and I sensed the lonely isolation that had been the bulk of his life so far. I asked him if anyone had come to visit him in the cave other than Ahnah. He shook his head.

"What about friends?" I asked. "Did you have any friends?"

Kata looked down at his grimy nails and repeated

the word, as if it were a lament.

I reached out to touch one of his big hands, but as I did so I felt a scratching at my collar, a familiar warm wriggling and a squeak, and then Victor emerged, blinking into the gloomy below-deck light.

Kata leapt backwards in alarm and Victor gave a frightened squeak. Kata stared at the sleepy mouseling; Victor gazed right back. Boy and mouse were both quivering.

"Don't be alarmed," I said to them both, lifting Victor gently from my shoulder and cupping his quivering form in my hand before extending it towards Kata. I felt Victor's heart rate quicken.

"Victor, this is my friend Kata."

I saw the boy's eyes leap to mine at the word.

"Kata, this is Victor. Don't be afraid; he won't bite." I recalled the encounter with Florenzo. "So long as you are gentle with him. Right, Victor?"

"Go on," I said to Kata.

The boy cautiously extended his own large fingers to mine. Then Victor – the braver of the two – looked back at me with a questioning expression before tiptoeing from my fingers on to the palm of Kata's hand.

The two stared at each other for a long moment and neither moved, then Victor gave one of his yawns and a wiggle, and Kata smiled.

"Good," I said. "Now that's out of the way we can all be friends."

Chapter 16

The voyage proceeded calmly but our progress was slow due to the storm damage. As Kata recovered, he and Victor and I spent many hours together. None of the other mariners would come near the cabin and Ishmael was still laid up with sickness, so we were free to amuse ourselves as we wished.

That first day I taught him noughts and crosses, and draughts, which we played with coloured pebbles on the dusty floor of his cage, Victor nudging the stones along with his nose. A few days later I borrowed a pack of cards from the Russian midshipman and we played snap and cheat and other games I had seen the mariners play in the quarterdeck. We talked of our families and our childhoods. It turned out we had much in common:

both of us having lost our mothers in childbirth, both brought up by a female relative, both longing to know absent fathers. It became clear that Kata had imagined his father as a traveller, an explorer, a great adventurer.

"Ahnah, she tell me of my father's travels," he said one morning. I had managed to steal a map from my father's cabin, intending to show Kata where I came from and where we were heading, but he wanted to see instead the location of his father's birthplace. Wondering what exactly he knew of his father's history, I showed him Inglestadt on the map and then Lake Geneva, a place he had heard his father talk of before he had disappeared.

"My grandfather was brought up there too," said Kata, looking at the blue shape on the map – the lake surrounded by mountains where Victor Frankenstein had indeed been born and raised. "He did my father a great wrong."

I looked at Kata and wondered how I had ever seen him as anything other than human. And now his words made me see the story of Victor Frankenstein and his creation differently too. For who was the greatest villain in the story – Kata's father, the scientist who created him, or the society that named him a monster?

I wanted to ask more – but just then the door of the

cabin opened and I saw my own father silhouetted in the doorway.

"What," he demanded, "is going on here?"

I was saddened by the change I saw in my father. He looked tired – more tired than I had ever seen him before. He stared at the sight before him: the cage door open; Kata and I seated within the iron bars, playing draughts; Victor perched on Kata's knee. He looked at me in confusion, then his gaze shifted to Kata, seeming at first unable to comprehend what he was looking at.

"Where is your father?" were the only words he could articulate.

My father took a step forward and Kata flinched.

"Where is he?"

Kata just shook his head. He was trembling, as if in anticipation of violence.

"When did you last see him?" Another uncertain step towards the open door of the cage.

Kata pressed himself into the far corner of the cage, curling his legs into a ball, as if trying to make himself as small as possible.

"When?" repeated my father, each syllable making Kata flinch. "Where? You must know where he is."

"He doesn't!" I cried. "He has never known his

father. He left when Kata was born."

"Kata?" My father's head twitched at the name.

"He's not a monster, Father. He's just a boy."

My father seemed to see me for the first time and his face filled with a new expression – love, fear, despair.

"Get out of the cage, Maggie," he whispered.

"Father!"

"I said get out of the cage. I can't see you hurt. He is dangerous."

"No, he's not. He's not like his father."

"Do as I say, Maggie," my father insisted, his voice no longer angry, just exhausted. "I am doing this for you. To give you a better life, a better future. I cannot … see you hurt."

"Kata will not hurt me," I said. "He is my friend."

"Get out of there, Maggie. Now!"

His tone was harsher than I had ever heard it. I jumped to my feet and, with one last apologetic look at Kata, I stepped out of the cage. My father slammed the door shut, turned the key and pocketed it.

There was a long pause. The anger seemed to seep out of my father as he appeared to reach the end of some complicated calculation. "You may continue to care for the creature," he told me. "But tell … your friend –" he struggled to articulate the word – "that if he does not provide information leading to the capture of his father, then this … friendship is at an end."

"But, Father—"

"And if he hurts you – if he lays a finger on you – I will send him to hell where Victor Frankenstein dwells!"

And with that my father left again, back to his cabin.

Neither of us spoke for some time. We were separated now by the bars of the cage, but also by my father's words. It was Victor who breached the gap, running from one of us to the other, nudging his nose against Kata's thumb then scampering back to do the same to mine, his warm scuttlings marking out an invisible thread of friendship running between us that no knife could sever.

"I – I am so sorry. My father … is … not himself."

"Why does he want to find my father?"

I tried to explain. About how the young impressionable Captain Walton had met Victor Frankenstein that fateful day in the Arctic. How he had faithfully recorded the scientist's story then watched him die. How he had seen the monster leap on to the bow of his ship and cradle his dead master in his arms.

"He has seen my father?" Kata crouched near where I sat, his fingers meeting mine through the bars.

"And your grandfather too."

"And is it true what the people said?" He hesitated. "That Victor Frankenstein created my father from pieces of dead men?"

I nodded.

"Is it true that my father was a … murderer? That he killed Victor Frankenstein's brother? His friend? His wife?"

I nodded though I knew it pained him.

"So my father was a murderer. My grandfather a devil," said Kata, his face dropping in sorrow. "What does that make me?"

Chapter 17

It took us nearly two weeks to reach New York. At the first sight of land I felt both elated and devastated. I was longing to taste something other than salt fish and ship's biscuit; I was desperate for a wash and a change of clothes; and yet over the journey, Kata had come to feel like family – and I feared America must bring our time together to an end.

My father had visited Kata no more. He seemed to have forgotten the threats, having turned to the bottle, spending all of his time rum-soaked and whisky-pickled in his chamber, refusing company or food. I had never feared for him as I did in those last days at sea.

Fortunately Ishmael had recovered and in the final days of the voyage he summoned me to his chamber, from which all had been barred save Queequeg the Second. "I hear that history repeats itself. Once again the beauty has befriended her beast," he said.

I looked at him in surprise. The sickness had wasted him and he seemed to have aged a thousand years on this journey.

"He is no beast, as certainly as I am no beauty," I said with a laugh.

"Only one of those statements is true," said the withered old sea dog. "But which one?"

"He is no monster," I insisted. "He is more like his mother than his father!"

"And what of you, Maggie? Are you like your father too?"

I had no time for such riddles. "What will happen to him when we get to New York?"

"I cannot leave the ship," said Ishmael, and I knew what he said was true. He was bound to the sea, just as my father was bound to his quest. He could not survive on land for longer than a few weeks – nay, a few hours – before the longing took him and he would have to set sail once more. "But if you or Kata need a friend in the city, seek out Madame La Barboule. She is a dear friend of mine," the ancient mariner continued. "Tell her Ishmael sent you and she will surely help."

"But how will I know her?"

"She is the most ladylike of women you will ever encounter," he said, offering no further explanation, but going on, "and if you are in real trouble, find this man."

The old captain handed me a slip of paper and I unfolded it. It was a Wanted poster, offering a reward of a hundred dollars for the recovery of one William Wraithmell: "Smuggler, Petty Thief, Cattle Rustler and Spy". The man in the picture had a face that could easily get lost in a crowd – a face like a hundred other faces, save for a scar that ran from his left eye to his earlobe.

"Who is he?"

"Some know him as Will Wraithmell, others as Enoch Crosby or Harvey Birch, others simply as Culpepper," said Ishmael. "Some say he was Washington's spy, others that he crossed his palm for the English. Perhaps both are true. But if you are in need, he will not fail you."

"How will I find him?"

"He will find you," said Ishmael with a smile as old as the seas.

I wanted to ask more but I knew that there was no point. I stared at Ishmael's leathery old face and wondered if I would ever see him again. "What will you do?" I asked.

"I'll keep sailing the seven seas till the oceans claim me or I sail off the end of the earth!" He laughed like a rusty nail drawn across glass. "Or perhaps I will return to the Inuit, and spend my last days in a house of snow, chasing walrus across the ice."

"Will you keep looking for Kata's father?"

Ishmael shook his head. "I have seen men swallowed in the belly of an obsession so deep it drives them to madness. I will not go there again. It is best your father believes the monster is dead."

"Believes? Do *you* think he might still live?"

Ishmael shrugged. "Do not allow yourself to be taken by the curse. Look after Kata. Set him free from it. Then live your life!"

Chapter 18

New York harbour was not so different from Shadwell Basin. As the ship came into dock, I recognised the familiar smells and sounds – and new sensations too. The twang of the voices, the aromas – spices, tobacco, the stench of human bodies. I saw a chain of slaves, tied together by manacles round their necks, staggering along the jetty, while a fat overseer, with a face like a bear, lunged at them with a whip. I had never seen slaves in such numbers before, herded together like cattle. I felt Victor shudder in my pocket.

Once the *Moby Dick* was safely moored my father sent word to Florenzo and the cage containing Kata was readied for disembarking. It was covered in a giant piece of sacking so that the contents were invisible, but word of our strange cargo had quickly spread, and a crowd of people assembled to watch the cage being lifted from the ship. This was done by a team of slaves, their skin marked with lines where they had been lashed, their ankles and wrists sore with the rings of shackles. From their wide eyes and fearful mumbling, it was clear they were afraid of their task, but they dared not refuse.

I stayed close by the cage as it was loaded on to rollers, and I heard the murmurs from the crowd as we passed down the gangplank and on to the jetty. Some said it was a polar bear, others that it was an abominable snowman, and still more believed it was a mermaid. All seemed to shrink back as we passed. Little did they realise the cage contained nothing more than a large, frightened child.

The cage was loaded on to a cart and taken through the streets of the city. I was excited to see this brave new world of America – the young nation that had fought for its independence and defeated a great empire. But if I had expected a metropolis like London, I was to be disappointed. New York was a younger, rougher, more vital city – sprung up with an energy like a rough weed fighting for its space in the sunshine. It lacked the grandeur of my native city – no building here was any older than Ishmael; the majority were younger than I was, built in an eclectic variety of styles, drawn no doubt from the mixed ancestry of the city's immigrant inhabitants. New York was young, scrappy and hungry, and I felt immediately at home.

The cart was carried through the cobbled streets until at last we approached a building in the Bowery district; a converted warehouse that bore a sign declaring "Florenzo's Circus of Curiosities". The red-brick walls bore posters with slogans such as "The Bearded Woman of Oregon", "The Hundred-Year-Old Dwarf" and "Siam's Finest Conjoined Twins".

I stared at the billboards in confusion as we stopped before the warehouse. What was this place? Florenzo had told my father that he was a man of science, but this was neither laboratory nor museum. I shivered with foreboding.

We were taken round the back of the building, and giant double doors swung open to let the cage in. I was aware of shadowy figures watching us as we were ushered through a gloomy tunnel, before emerging into the light of a circular arena, strewn with sawdust and surrounded on all sides by crude wooden seating that rose up in tiers daubed in gaudy colours, the paint peeling, and once bright flags of bunting hanging limp

103

and faded in desolate triangles.

The team of slaves departed, leaving just my father and me standing on either side of the cage. Victor had disappeared into his pouch.

"Are you all right?" I whispered to Kata.

No answer.

A twitch in my pocket made me look up. From the other side of the ring approached the all-too-familiar figure of Count Florenzo. Familiar yet different. For he was dressed not in the solemn, inky tailoring he had worn in London, but in the scarlet insignia of the circus master – red tailcoat, golden hessians, gleaming top boots, an ebony stovepipe hat – and he bore a pearl-topped cane, which he twirled around in his hand like a baton.

His face was lit by a strange and terrifying glee.

"Welcome!" he cried. "To Florenzo's Circus of Curiosities!"

He raised his arms and gestured flamboyantly. "Roll up, roll up for the greatest show on earth. Prepare to be amazed by the celebrated bearded mermaid, the two-hundred-year-old woman! See the world's smallest strongman and the extraordinary conjoined twins – too miraculous to behold!"

I could hear Kata's shuddering breaths and felt

Victor scuttle from his pouch, wriggle his way down my leg and slip quickly under the canvas to join the frightened boy.

"What do you think of my kingdom?" cried Florenzo. "Is it not the finest spectacle in New York?"

"You said you were a man of science!" my father said in a horrified whisper.

"The science of entertainment!" said Florenzo. "The greatest science of them all!"

My father's face, etched already with lines of horror and disappointment, turned an ashy white.

"So, Walton," Florenzo went on, his eyes staring greedily at the crate, "did you bring me my monster?"

"You said you were in pursuit of the source of life," my father muttered. "You wanted to discover the antidote to death…"

"How I have longed to behold it," Florenzo went on, ignoring him. "How I have dreamed of this moment – of seeing the man-made man in the flesh!"

"I only did this – only brought you this child – to save lives," my father muttered. "End suffering…"

"Let me behold it!" Florenzo was in front of the cage and I stepped forward to try to stop him, but I was too late. He pulled away the canvas cover with a flourish, then stopped.

Kata was crouched in the back of the crate, eyes wide with fright. I could just see Victor perched by his ear.

There was a long moment's silence.

"What. Is. This?"

I had invested some effort in ensuring that Kata was presentable for this encounter, insisting he was thoroughly clean from head to toe, cutting his shaggy hair from out of his eyes, clipping his fingernails and dressing him in what fresh clothing we could fashion from the ripped mainsail. As a result, he looked like a child – a large child with a scarred face – but certainly no monster. And the sight seemed to appal Florenzo.

"Where is my creature?"

My father muttered just a single syllable. "Dead."

"Dead?" Florenzo's eyes glittered like the pearl that twinkled at the top of his cane.

"All believe it has perished," said my father, who seemed suddenly childlike in the face of Florenzo's wrath – a schoolboy who had not completed his homework, "many years since."

"I don't believe it!" cried Florenzo, his voice becoming more heavily accented as his anger rose. "I will not believe it! I paid you to bring me the monster! Where is my monster?"

"I have brought you something different," my father

stammered. "Something better. I have bought you the monster's child."

"The ... child?" Florenzo's eyes had taken on a crazed expression as his gaze flickered back to Kata's crouched form.

"The monster sired him," stammered my father. "A thing with no life created new life. This ... is the scientific miracle you paid me to bring back."

My father gestured at Kata, who was curled up, terrified, at the back of the cage. He did not look like an abomination. His features may have been strange, but the light in his eyes was so gentle, so fearful, so human.

Florenzo spoke in a voice that was dangerously quiet. "You tell me this overgrown child is the monster's boy?"

"Yes. By an English girl with whom it fell in love."

"That murderous beast was not capable of love!" hissed the count.

"Call it what you will," said my father, growing in desperation – recalling, perhaps, all he had staked on the success of this mission. "It is the child's father."

Florenzo was staring at Kata now, the fury remaining in his eyes. But I saw a host of other emotions cross over his face too – dawning comprehension, and then a flicker of excitement, succeeded by something darker, deeper, more intense. He held Kata's gaze and I saw my friend shiver.

Then the ringmaster turned to my father, his tone icy-cold. "We made a deal, Walton. You were to bring me the monster and take a share in the spoils. And if you failed…"

"I—"

"If you failed, the whole cost of the enterprise fell to you."

His words fell like hammers. I had no idea that my father had staked so much. His voice, when he spoke, was barely a whisper. "But I brought you this…"

"*This* is not the creation of Victor Frankenstein," said Florenzo. "*This* is not the bounty you bound yourself to provide."

My father stared at him. "But the monster is dead!"

"No!" Kata spoke for the first time, the single syllable making all turn in his direction.

"What did you say?"

"My father is alive." Kata's brown eyes were wide, but he held Florenzo's stare without flinching. "And he will come and get me!"

Chapter 19

Florenzo ordered the cage to be wheeled into the vast space behind the arena, and it was here that I saw the true nature of the place to which we had been brought. I gazed at the paraphernalia of Florenzo's circus – silken drapes, fiery hoops, a human cannon, a trapeze – surrounded by cages of exotic animals from far-flung corners of the globe – a camel, a caged tiger, a white stallion with a horn crudely attached to make it appear a unicorn. And, most surprising of all, the circus performers who emerged slowly from the shadows, dressed in the most extraordinary assortment of outfits I had ever seen.

There was a tiny strongman, perhaps three feet tall, dressed in a wrestler's leotard emblazoned with sparkling stars and stripes; a pair of conjoined twins in an extraordinary double ball gown that made them look like a two-headed goddess; an old man with a neck as long as a giraffe's and encircled with golden rings; acrobats and tumblers of all shapes and sizes with gaudily painted faces and outfits encrusted with paste gems. Most striking of all was a creature who resembled a mermaid – shining silver scales shimmering down lower limbs that fused together to create a fish tail, golden hair cascading down her shoulders and … a healthy beard upon her face.

"Madame La Barboule?"

The beautiful vision looked most surprised. "That is me, child. How do you know my name?"

"I was told to look for you. By Captain Ishmael."

"Ishmael?" Again the beauty's face changed. Her voice rose and fell like a sea creature slipping through deeps and shallows. "What did that old sea dog have to say of me?"

"He said you were the most ladylike creature he had ever set eyes upon, and that I should know you at once by that description."

Madame La Barboule closed her eyes for a second and a faint flush seemed to accompany the sad smile on ruby lips just visible beneath the golden beard.

"Ever the gentleman, Ishmael," she said. "The captain and I undertook many a journey together. We both know something of the call of the other side." She seemed to be speaking in a kind of code that I could not decipher and which I suspected was not intended for me. "And he sent you to me, did he?"

The others had been staring at Kata throughout this exchange, and at this point the little strongman piped up. "Begging your pardon, miss, but we was expecting something a little … bigger?"

"They said he was half man, half monster!" said one of the conjoined twins.

"Half living, half dead," said the other.

"Half devil, half human," added a young girl who was covered from head to foot with hair.

"Aren't we all, darling!" said Madame La Barboule.

She silenced a muttered response with a single wave of her many-ringed hand.

"Come now, who are any of us to judge the boy's appearance?" said the bearded mermaid. "We are a community of 'others'– here to dazzle and delight, to horrify audiences and remind them of their humanity. For why else do they come to the circus? We reassure them they are not alone."

The collection of performers muttered some more,

but none protested, though they continued to stare at Kata. I could not see Victor but suspected that he had curled himself next to Kata's heart as he did for me when I needed him most.

"Is that what Florenzo wants Kata for?" I asked. "To perform?"

"It's the only thing we are good for, darling!" said Madame La Barboule. "To the world, we are monsters. But on stage, it loves us. And the ringmaster has great plans for the new arrival. Look!"

She drew a freshly made poster from a pile lying on one of the wicker cases nearby. I stared at the brightly coloured playbill as she waved it in the air. "Come See the Man-Made Monster!" it declared in sweeping letters. "The Corpse Creature brought from the Dead by the Power of UnGodly Galvanism!" There was a crudely painted picture of what I supposed was intended to be Kata's father – raven-haired, yellow-eyed, crackling with bolts of lightning.

"He was to be Florenzo's biggest attraction!" said the little strongman.

"Crowds would throng to see him," said a tiny, beautiful acrobat girl dressed in a sequinned leotard.

"But Kata doesn't want to be paraded in front of the world!" I said.

"Do you think any of us wants that?" asked the giraffe-necked old man, hair as white as snow, earlobes hanging almost to his shoulders. "Florenzo gives us no choice."

"And people must be amused," said Madame La Barboule. "So reserve your judgement, Maggie Walton, and make the best of us, not the worst."

Chapter 20

And so it was that Kata and my father and I joined the company of Florenzo's Circus of Curiosities. The community of performers welcomed us, and Kata and I quickly found our place among them. Everyone had to work in the circus, and now that my father was entirely beholden to Florenzo, that meant me too. So with the help of the tiny ballerina, whose name was Mignon, Victor and I developed our own act – "Mistress Maggie and her Magical Mouse" – which involved Victor performing tricks to my command. We were to circulate among the audience before the show, entertaining with our antics and collecting coppers for our efforts.

My father was put to work too, and this was a less

happy affair. He was indentured to Florenzo until he paid off his debt – a life sentence. The agony of seeing what he had condemned me to would have surely been enough to break my father – yet the count seemed determined to humiliate him further. So he was dressed in a clownish suit, his face painted like the great Grimaldi, and a tray of popcorn slung round his neck to sell to the crowds. Not only this, but he had to wear a placard that bore the command, "Popcorn and a Punch", encouraging all customers to land a blow upon the vendor. And so my brilliant father – poet, scientist, explorer, philosopher – was sunk to the status of a common hawker; drunken louts queuing up to land punches, which he received with a tame indifference that broke my heart.

For since our arrival at the circus he seemed a shattered man. A deep melancholy seemed to weigh him down, and despair at the fate he had consigned us to ate at him like a cancer. "I never meant this for you!" he would say over and over. "Forgive me, Maggie."

He was tortured, too, by what Florenzo had in mind for Kata. The showman's initial disappointment had transformed into something even more unnerving, for after locking himself away in his office for nearly two whole days after our arrival, he emerged with eyes that glistened oddly and a sheaf of papers clutched in his hand that he waved triumphantly before the cage in which Kata was still imprisoned.

"I am going to make you a star!" he declared, a light in his eyes that I could only describe as ungodly. "The greatest star New York – nay, the world – has ever seen!"

His plan for stardom involved an act that seemed ghoulish to me, but which Florenzo believed would enthral the crowds. Florenzo had in his possession a version of Victor Frankenstein's story – not the letters that my aunt had instructed me to burn, but a faithful account of the story by another hand. And this formed the basis of his act. Florenzo himself was to play the role of Victor Frankenstein, to tell the story of the Genevan scientist's colossal arrogance and ambition, of how he had set himself up as a god, capable of bestowing life, usurping the role of the Almighty himself – and how he had built a monster.

Then Kata was to be wheeled on to the stage, prostrate, tied down by iron shackles to what resembled a surgeon's operating table. La Barboule would employ her make-up skills to give my friend a positively ghoulish appearance, and the conjoined twins – Mawu and Lisa, named for the goddesses of the moon and sun – who were talented seamstresses, had devised clothing to exaggerate his colossal size. Florenzo, meanwhile, had fashioned a giant golden wand with which he would pretend to apply the electric current to Kata's inert form and give the appearance of awakening him from the dead. This was to be accompanied by whizzes and bangs and lots of smoke, devised by the giraffe-necked man, whose name was Lae Khoe, and who hailed from a Myanmar people famed for their knowledge of the pyrotechnic arts.

"The audience will love it!" declared Florenzo. "A story of ambition and abandonment that will echo down the ages."

"I don't like it," I told Kata.

"It is my father's story," said Kata, who was happier than I to trust the showman. Perhaps it was the allure of the circus, or perhaps the obsessive attention Florenzo lavished upon his star act as they prepared for the opening night; or perhaps it was the appeal of enacting his father's story, for Kata did not mind his role in the Gothic horror show Florenzo had devised. And yet I could not quell my unease.

"The crowd will love it, of course," said La Barboule as the day for unveiling the new act dawned.

"And we all know how Florenzo loves to please the crowd!" said Lae Khoe, who told me he had been chief of the whole Kayan nation of people before traders sold him to the circus.

"And yet it feels more than that," said La Barboule as she and Mignon applied the ghoulish make-up to Kata's cheeks, covering up a nasty bruise from an accident in rehearsal when one of the explosions had gone off too close to his face. "It feels…"

"Personal," I finished the sentence for her.

"Yes," she said, her soft grey eyes filled with sadness as she looked at the bruise flowering on Kata's cheek. "I have known Florenzo many years; I know him to be heartless and mercenary. I know he is happy to exploit otherness to fill his purse. I know he cares not a jot for any of us. But I have never seen him like this."

"In rehearsal his eyes are on fire with joy," said Lae Khoe.

"Yes, it is personal with him," said Madame La Barboule. "And so – who knows…"

Victor had jumped on to Kata's shoulder and was gently licking his bruised cheek.

"When I first met him he was different," said La Barboule with a faraway look in her mermaid eyes. "We met on board Ahab's ship long, long ago. Florenzo was searching for something even then – but not the monster. It was a woman he sought. He was a poor man, down on his luck, but there was something about him…"

She paused now, a smile flitting across her face. A hush had fallen, like that when she appeared on stage, glimmering in a giant oyster shell, singing like a siren to bring the audience under her spell. "He made me believe he loved me. Perhaps he even did – a little."

I stared at her in surprise.

"He persuaded me to come with him to New York," she said, ruby lips curling in a soft smile. "He told me America was a new world where class, race, colour, gender did not matter; where a man, or woman – or anyone – could be accepted. I trusted him, perhaps because I was young and in love. I wanted to believe in the existence of such a world. And so I followed him."

"What happened?" asked Mignon.

"When we landed in New York it all changed," said the mermaid with the saddest of all smiles. "He displayed me as a curio in coffee shops and saloons and gin bars and other such low venues. He told me it was just till we had enough money to settle down, but I'm not sure he ever intended otherwise."

The look on her face was now a picture of heartbreak. Kata's wound was visible, his bruise flowering there for all to see – but hers was written just as clearly on her face.

"He was a good businessman, I'll say that for him," she said with a toss of her golden hair. "If he had ever felt anything for me, it was soon eclipsed by the shimmer of gold. I became a commodity to him. He began to scour the city for other "curiosities". He found the strongman Enano indentured in the Meatpacking District; Lae Khoe half dead in a slave boat down by the docks; Mignon begging in Central Park."

Each nodded in silent recollection.

"Then Florenzo bought a wagon and took us all around the country, stopping at every village and mining settlement, every frontier town. He'd put up a tent and charge a few cents for folks to see his bearded lady, his giraffe man, his weight-lifting dwarf. And along the way he'd collect more desperate outcasts."

"He found us in Buffalo," said Mawu.

Her twin Lisa added, "Our parents had left us in an orphanage."

"I was starving under a bush in Wyoming," said the hairy girl, who had no name when she joined the troupe and was now called Rapunzel.

"But it always felt as if he were looking for something – someone – else. He seemed never to find what he was really in search of. And there grew a darkness in his

120

soul that no amount of money could fill."

"And he made a *lot* of money," said Enano. "Though we didn't see much of it! We are all indentured – we all belong to him. We are little better than slaves."

"We returned to New York and he set up the emporium," said La Barboule. "It made him happy at first. Until one day last year he received a parcel containing a bundle of notebooks."

"Who were they from?"

"Mignon saw the man who brought them – a Frenchman, she said, or a German, fresh off the boat. And I saw the journals on the desk in his office once – old, the parchment yellowing. It was as if a fever that had lain dormant in his blood suddenly reignited. He set off for England to find your father, Maggie, and he returned so happy, so hopeful, that I almost recognised the man I had fallen in love with." She paused for a moment, fingering a strand of golden hair. "I think he believed that finding the monster would bring him peace, set to rest the demons that had haunted him, allow him to be who he had once been … to love again."

"But then we didn't find the monster," I said.

"No," said La Barboule. She shook her beautiful mane of hair and heaved a profound sigh. "I wonder if it would have been any different if you had."

Chapter 21

The audience loved the new act.

For Kata it was not so much fun.

Posters all over New York billed it as "The Greatest Spectacle on Earth: Watch the Dead Man Walk! See the Birth of a Monster! Witness a Modern Prometheus!" The audience came ready to be amazed; whether they expected mere theatrics or a true modern miracle, who can say, but they flocked in droves to see the electric man.

And Florenzo's showmanship did not disappoint. The act was last on the bill; after the strongmen, the acrobats, the bearded mermaid and the conjoined twins had wowed the crowds, Florenzo took centre stage, dressed in a new suit of gleaming gold and ruby, his eyes reflecting the scarlet hue of the cloth as he began to tell the tale I had recounted so many times to the children of the Basin.

The audience were as transfixed as Jenny Stocking and Tommy Tucker and the little match girl had been. They ooh-ed and ah-ed as Florenzo narrated the ghoulish prologue, then roared their approval as Kata's inert form was wheeled on. La Barboule's make-up was a work of art, as was the outfit the twins had fashioned for him, and under the gaslights Kata truly did look monstrous. Men booed and hissed, children pointed, women screamed.

Florenzo held his golden wand aloft.

But it was not the same one he had used during rehearsals. This was connected to long cables that stretched from the ceiling and hummed dangerously as he approached the bench.

"I collected the instruments of life around me," Florenzo was saying. The wand sparked in his hand and I saw him bring it close to Kata's temple.

"I would infuse a spark of being into the lifeless thing that lay before me!"

Suddenly I knew what he was going to do but I stood there paralysed, unable to move.

And then the golden wand was at Kata's temple,

and, instead of the theatrical whizzes and bangs that had been rehearsed, a bolt of pure lightning shot down the cables and through the metal shaft into my friend's skull.

"No!" I heard myself cry out. I tried to spring forward but I felt strong arms holding me back.

I saw the glee on Florenzo's face, I saw the spark, I heard Kata scream in horror, I watched his whole body convulse in agony. I heard myself cry out again; I heard the audience gasp.

"The dull yellow eye of the creature opened," Florenzo was declaiming, the prepared script delivered as an elated incantation. "The creature lurched to its feet and I beheld the wretch, the miserable monster I had created."

Kata attempted to get up but another shot of electricity threw him down at Florenzo's feet.

"No!" I sobbed. "No!"

"His jaws opened and he muttered some inarticulate sounds," cried the count, his face crazed with a wild joy as another bolt of electricity caused Kata to wail in agony.

"We have to stop him!" I sobbed, turning frantically to Madame La Barboule, whose strong arms held me back, and to my fellow performers, who stood – as horrified as I – watching from the wings. "Somebody has to stop him!"

Kata was stumbling drunkenly now, and every time he tried to get to his feet Florenzo sent another shock through his limbs. He seemed dazed, disorientated, his face twisted in pain and disappointment.

"We cannot stop him!" said Madame La Barboule. "If we try, it will be worse for Kata."

The act was nearly over. They had rehearsed a climax that saw the monster defeated, a broken creature at Florenzo's feet. This time it was no act. Kata crawled on hands and knees, his eyes pleading, and Florenzo held aloft the electric wand, crying, "And thus I destroyed the demoniacal corpse to which I had so miserably given life!"

A final shot of electricity, a ghoulish howl from Kata, an eruption of applause from the audience and it was all over.

And I had no idea if my friend was alive or dead.

Chapter 22

"**I** have never seen the audience like this," said Madame La Barboule as Kata was carried off stage. He was breathing – just – but his motionless body was marked with bruises and cuts and burn marks.

"They bayed like animals!" said Lae Khoe. "Hungry to see more pain."

"Kata!" I cried, kneeling at his side and cradling his head, willing him to wake up.

He opened one eye; the other was too swollen. "Maggie?"

"What has he done to you?"

"I am … fine!" It came out as barely a croak.

"No, you're not!" I said, staring at the dark burn marks on his temples, his cheeks, his neck. "How could he do this?"

"He can do it because Kata belongs to him. The contract Florenzo signed with your father entitled him to all the spoils of the voyage," said Enano, who had carried Kata's body from the ring.

"But there must be some law?"

"The law will not lift a finger against a man who disciplines his property – his slaves," said La Barboule. "And that is what he is in the eyes of the law."

The word struck me like a blow. Property.

"Then we have to get Kata away from here!" My mind was whirring frantically. "We can run away somewhere he could never find us."

La Barboule shook her head. "Your father is not well enough," she said. "And if you run he will punish the captain."

I knew she was right. My father was too weak to attempt escape.

"Then what?" I asked desperately. "What can we do?"

Chapter 23

There was nothing we could do. Kata's act was a success – a roaring success. Box-office takings had tripled and the "electrified corpse" was the talk of the town. Florenzo was in an ecstasy during each performance, and Kata endured it all with a quiet stoicism born of a lifetime of suffering. But I could not bear it.

And now the crowds had a taste for blood, their appetite grew every day more monstrous, more ravenous.

"I don't like it!" said Enano, who had seen horrors in the Meatpacking District but none that compared to this. "It makes the crowd mean. The other day I dropped the dumb-bells on my foot and I got the biggest cheer in the show. They used to revel in my success – now they pray for my downfall."

"Did you hear them boo and heckle the twins last night?" asked one of the acrobats who juggled fire and swallowed flames. "They used to ooh and ah. Now they bay for blood!"

Blood was good for business, it seemed, for through the streets of New York the message spread – "Come see the man monster – watch him howl!" and audiences poured in. From Manhattan came the well-heeled elite; from the Bowery came the drunks and bums; from Queens and the Meatpacking District came the workers who spent all day in the docks and the slaughterhouses. They wanted their nights lit with a little magic, their hearts cheered by acts of wonder and daring, their deeper desires satisfied with a little cruelty.

And Florenzo was happy to oblige. Each night, the act with Kata got a little longer, a little meaner, a little crueller. Each night, Kata came off with more wounds for me to tend, and still the crowds cried, "Encore! Encore! More! More! More!"

"He can't keep doing this!" I said after a particularly punishing show that had left Kata whimpering in a heap in the middle of the sawdust ring, blood pouring from his head. "Somebody needs to stop Florenzo before he kills you."

Kata looked at me through the one eye that was not sealed shut with bruising. "Maybe that is what he wants."

"No, he won't kill his biggest attraction," said Enano.

"Then why does he hurt him so!" asked the little ballerina, Mignon, who cried each night when Kata came off stage in his pitiful state.

"If we could find out, then maybe we could figure out a way to make him stop," I said.

"Maybe," said La Barboule doubtfully.

"I have to try at least!" I said. "Before he goes too far!"

Chapter 24

I spent the next few days trying to devise ways to get into Florenzo's office. He always kept it carefully locked, the key slung on a chain round his neck. I concocted all sorts of outlandish plans: picking locks with a hairpin, plucking the key from him using a giant magnet, or digging a tunnel to emerge beneath his desk. In the end none was needed, for an escaped tiger caused him to leave the office door unlocked and I was able to dart inside.

And what I beheld alarmed me so, I almost wished I had not witnessed it.

Every inch of the office walls was covered with newspaper cuttings, diagrams, sheaves of paper. All relating to Victor Frankenstein. To the monster. To my father. And to Kata.

There were faded sheets covered in spidery handwriting, the story of Frankenstein and his creation told within them. There were sketches that claimed to depict the "monster". And newspaper cuttings – some about the death of William Frankenstein, Victor's young brother, and the trial of Justine Moritz, who had been convicted of his murder; some reporting the brutal slaughter of Henry Clerval, Frankenstein's best friend.

My attention was caught by an article that lay on Florenzo's desk: an obituary – a death notice in the London *Times*. The picture of the deceased gazed out at me. Dark-haired, with large almond eyes. Elizabeth Frankenstein – beloved wife and daughter. The verdict: death by misadventure. No mention of the brutal means of her demise. A brief reference to her history – "Adopted by Victor Frankenstein's parents after her abandonment by her own father, an Italian nobleman fallen into disgrace". The piece was yellowing with age, clearly well thumbed.

"Why would he keep all of this?" I asked Victor, who had scuttled down on to the desk and was staring at the woman's face on the yellowing paper.

I glanced around the office to find an answer. There

was a wall dedicated to scientific articles – new discoveries in electricity, Galvani's experiments, gruesome images of electrical prods attached to twitching frogs' legs, and reanimated corpses. And another wall on which were pages and pages of sketches of Kata's act. I saw the costume, the table, the electric wand. And then I spotted some new sketch that depicted another figure in the act. A new costume idea. It looked like a wedding dress…

At that moment Victor emitted a loud squeak and I heard the sound of Florenzo's voice, and footsteps approaching.

I quickly stole an image from the wall, shoved it into my pocket and darted out of the room.

I had seen enough. More than enough!

Chapter 25

The newspapers had begun to decry the act as a fake. "Florenzo's corpse not really dead," said one. Another called for him to prove Kata was indeed awoken from the grave: "Run him through with a knife, cut him open on stage and show his unbeating heart," demanded the journalists. Some called for eminent scientists to verify the authenticity of the act, one newspaper even proposing that this be carried out in a surgeon's operating theatre.

There had been other demands too. Did not the story say that the monster killed young William Frankenstein, the inventor's brother? That he also took the life of Henry Clerval, Victor's dearest friend? Audiences wanted to see those bloody acts on stage too. But most of all they wished to see the murder of Elizabeth. This was the topic of conversation among the circus troupe when I returned, the tiger now returned to its cage, the mystery of its escape unresolved (though Enano – who had a mysterious new set of scratches upon his arms – winked conspiratorially in my direction).

"The more grisly horror the audience sees, the more their appetite for it grows," Madame La Barboule was saying. "Where will it end?"

"I know where!" I said, breathless. "In his office. I saw plans … for a new act."

"Heaven defend us! What does he have in mind for Kata now?"

"Not just for Kata."

But I did not have the chance to continue because just then Florenzo himself appeared, dressed in the ringmaster's gold and scarlet, which he seemed to have slept in, for he was dishevelled, his jacket unbuttoned, his eyes alight with the ungodly fire that I had seen in them before. "Where is Mignon?" he demanded.

The beautiful girl stepped forward, trembling. I could feel the paper in my pocket, see the drawings upon it. I knew immediately what he was going to say.

"You shall play Elizabeth in tonight's show."

"Elizabeth…?"

"Elizabeth Frankenstein," said Florenzo. "The people want to see the death of the most pure and beautiful maiden to step on this earth and we will show it to them."

"No!"

Madame La Barboule laid a hand on his arm, but Florenzo shook her off.

"Elizabeth was an angel. The creature ripped out her heart." His voice was alive with desire and cruelty. "I have seen it in my dreams, in my every waking thought. This act will be the greatest ever played on any stage!"

Victor, who was nestled in my pocket next to the paper, gave a squeak of alarm.

"It – it can't be safe!"

"Safe?" demanded Florenzo. "True art is not safe; true art takes risks, it dares, it aspires. The people of New York want horror. We will show them how he ripped the life from the dearest girl alive."

Mignon was white with shock. Kata looked as if he were going to be sick.

"I ... I won't do it," he said. "Do what you will to me, hurt me however you wish, but do not ask me to inflict pain on another."

Mignon turned her large grey eyes upon him with a look of gratitude that must surely have melted the heart of any but Count Florenzo.

"You are my creation to do with as I please." Florenzo's eyes ran over the wounds he had inflicted, as if Kata were an artwork, the wounds his brushstrokes. "You will do as I tell you or suffer the consequences."

"Then I will suffer them," said Kata, fearful but unabashed. "But do not ask me to hurt Mignon."

I saw the look that passed between Kata and Mignon, and felt something leap in my breast that I could neither recognise nor begin to name.

Florenzo's eyes bored into Kata as if he would enter his very soul, then he let out a low sinister laugh.

"Of course! I should have realised! To hurt the girl will cause you more pain than any whips and lashes."

For some reason Florenzo's statement caused another pang in my heart that felt like bolts of electricity.

"How gratifying," said Florenzo. "This will pack the turnstiles! Love and pain. How do you say it in England? Two birds with the one pebble."

Everyone was looking at the count. Mignon trembled in Madame La Barboule's arms; the troupe looked on in ghastly anticipation. I felt only a desperate sadness.

"I'll do it," I said.

Victor squeaked in alarm and ran up on to my shoulder.

"I will play Elizabeth. I know I am not as beautiful, nor as pure and good as Mignon, but if I get hurt it doesn't matter. Why risk your ballerina?"

"Maggie, no," said Kata. But I did not even look at him.

"You have a point," said Florenzo. He was staring, trying perhaps to see the face of the long-lost Elizabeth. The face of the girl in the newspaper cutting. A face ten times more beautiful than I could ever be. "It might be useful to have a spare – just in case…"

"I won't do this!" insisted Kata. "Maggie—"

"The time for discussion is over," said Florenzo with a wave of his white-gloved hand. "It is settled. I have already informed the press. The new act begins tonight."

Chapter 26

The clothes I wore were oddly old-fashioned. I don't know where Florenzo had procured a bridal gown in the antiquated Genevan style, but this is what I was dressed in, my hair delicately piled on my head and small pearl earrings clipped on my lobes. Madame La Barboule applied rouge to my lips and cheeks, so that when I looked in the mirror I hardly recognised myself. In the gaslight I was the ghost of a girl long gone, another victim of the monster who had blighted the lives of so many.

"You look…" Kata was staring at me with a strange expression on his battered face. "Nice."

"Thank you," I said, a little stiffly. "Mignon would have looked more beautiful."

Victor, nestled at my breast, snuggled closer.

"I don't want to do this," said Kata.

"Don't worry," I said with a shrug. "I'm tough. Much less breakable than Mignon."

"Maggie, please…"

I started to walk away. "Just do as Florenzo says and it will all be fine."

"Maggie, no!"

I turned to see not Kata but my father speaking. He beheld me with such misery it stopped me in my tracks, where Kata's words had not.

"I should have protected you from this."

"No! This is not your fault, Father. I just – I have to do this. I want to."

"I could never forgive myself if—"

"Don't worry, Father!" I told him. "All will be well!"

I think I even believed those words as I spoke them. But I was wrong.

By the time I was pushed on stage, Florenzo had already whipped up the crowd into a fury. They were incensed with tales of heinous crimes, seduced by the cruelty they had seen enacted on to Kata's flesh, enraged by his passive response, desperate to see bloodshed, to hear more screams. So when I appeared in the gaslights, luminous in white and holding a bridal bouquet, the crowd roared for violence. In the moments that followed, Florenzo narrated the tale of the monster of Frankenstein stealing into the bridal suite, seeking out his creator's new bride on their wedding night, ending her life and Frankenstein's happiness in one devastating blow. The whole crowd breathed with the same monstrous desire, the same vengeful fury, their moral indignation mixed with an equally potent desire for revenge. They wanted blood for blood – and if it was my blood for Elizabeth's, so be it.

"You need to stay here, Victor," I said, lifting my little friend gently on to the bridal bouquet. Victor squeaked in protest but I ignored him and took my place on the bed centre stage.

Florenzo used the electric wand to make Kata move towards me. Powerless to resist, he staggered closer, his movements jolting, every bolt of electricity making him lurch and twitch. He was nearly upon me, and I had never till this moment considered how big Kata was, how easily he could crush me with one single blow. I had always felt safe with him, but now, in the middle of the ring, the crowd baying for my blood, I was – for the first time – frightened of my friend.

Florenzo was right behind Kata now, the electric prod held to his neck as he bellowed, "He took her by the throat!"

I could have recited the words off by heart. This was the tale I had told to Tommy Tucker and Jenny Stocking and the little match girl down in the Basin. I knew exactly how this story ended.

"He took her by the throat," Florenzo repeated. Kata's face contorted but he did not move.

"He put his giant hands round her slender neck!" The crowd were baying for Kata to hurt me.

"Do it," I said. He was so close to me now that I could see every sinew in his body was fighting the current that ran through him.

Florenzo lifted the wand to Kata's temple. Kata cried out but still did not move.

"Do it," cried Florenzo. "He put his giant hands round her slender neck and wrung the life out of her..."

Again the crowd bayed, again the probe send bolts of fury through Kata's head, making his eyeballs roll in his skull. Again Kata lurched forward and I braced myself for the onslaught. He stumbled, his face contorted in pain, but held himself back. Again the probe was applied – Florenzo held it longer than I have ever seen. Kata's eyes rolled backwards and his cry of pain became an animal mewling.

The crowd were on their feet: every man, woman and child wanted to see Kata hurt me.

"Do it!" cried Florenzo, and the wand was again on Kata's neck. For a second our eyes met and I silently pleaded with him to hurt me, to make his nightmare stop, to end his pain. But he would not do it. The electricity fired once more and he staggered, his legs giving way, falling crumpled to the floor, twitching, inert, eyes two white globes rolling in his skull. I fell upon his body, sobbing as the crowd booed and hissed in anger.

Chapter 27

"We need to get you away from here."

It was Madame La Barboule whose words were the first I registered in the chaos that ensued. The show was over after that. I barely remembered how we got off stage, hurried away from the crowd who wanted to rip me apart with their own bare hands – and from Florenzo, who would happily have done the same.

"This is not about the show any more," said Madame La Barboule. "It is a vendetta."

Kata was slowly coming round from the severest blows he had ever received. Mignon tended to him with such adoration that it hurt me to see. La Barboule was right – this had gone beyond pleasing an audience.

"But Florenzo will never let us go!"

144

"I wasn't thinking of asking his permission!" said the bearded mermaid. "Kata will not be safe if you stay. He will not let him live after this."

"But where will we go?"

We had been at the circus for less than a month, and yet despite the horrors we had experienced, it felt more like home than any place I had known. I fitted in here with these people. I glanced at Kata and knew the same was true for him. "This is our home."

Madame La Barboule beheld me with a look that reminded me of my late aunt, then she sighed. "You have to leave. I have made contact with Wraithmell."

"Will Wraithmell?" I remembered the Wanted poster the old sea captain had thrust into my hand on the *Moby Dick*. "The man Ishmael mentioned?"

"The very same. He is another ... old friend. He can help you get out of New York, but first we need to get you out of the circus."

"But I can't leave my father!"

"I will care for him myself," said La Barboule.

I glanced at the mermaid and knew that she would do as she promised. She was one of the few people my father would talk to, and sometimes, when she cleaned up his face after yet another popcorn punch, I saw an expression in her eyes like that when she spoke about

Florenzo. After all, hadn't she once said that she had a tender heart for lost causes?

"He is the only family I have." Victor emitted an indignant squeak. "Except Victor, of course."

"And us," said Mignon.

"All of us," added the twins.

I looked around at the troupe of Curiosities – little Enano, long-necked old Lae Khoe, the bearded Rapunzel. They were all smiling and nodding. They were all accepting me into their family.

And telling me that I had to leave it forever.

I wanted to cry, but instead I gulped back the tears that threatened to fall and asked, "How will we escape without Florenzo catching us?"

Lae Khoe grinned. "We need a little bit of theatre!"

Chapter 28

The escape was planned for the next night. Everyone was in on the scheme – except my father. And it involved fire.

Enano and the troupe of acrobats had a flamethrowing act with flaming dumb-bells and fiery hoops that appeared on the bill just before the Frankenstein act. Madame La Barboule had called on her contacts on the dockside to procure some barrels of a substance named "Abigail Adam's Finest", which Lae Khoe would fashion into something called "fire lances", which he said were commonly used by his people in Myanmar.

And thus the plan was set. Kata and I had our few belongings packed, along with some provisions for the first few days of our journey: a few bits of clothing, some food and money La Barboule had put aside "for a rainy day". Each of the troupe had donated a few coins, a bit of food, and small gifts to remember them by ("Or to sell if you need to eat!" Enano said with typical practicality). Mignon had given a copper bracelet that she had been wearing when she was found under the bush in Missouri, and which she believed had been given to her by her long-lost parents; Enano donated a gold medal from a dead Cherokee warrior that he had found in the meatpacking factory; Lae Khoe gave a hollowed-out tube and a box of tiny arrow-shaped pellets that he said was a poison blowgun that could knock out a man for two whole days (and a tiger for an hour); and Madame La Barboule gave us a beautiful conch shell, swirled with pinks and coral and pearlescent white, which she said had been given to her by a real mermaid. These, along with an assortment of other small tokens and trifles from other members of Florenzo's emporium, were wrapped into our bundles and laid by the back door, ready for departure when the moment came.

The touchpaper was lit towards the end of the firethrower's display. The audience was ooh-ing and aah-ing at the pyrotechnics when Florenzo appeared backstage. "Don't even think of backing out this time, monster-boy," he told Kata with a dangerous snarl. "For if you won't hurt the girl, then be sure that I will!"

He raised the electric wand in the air with a flourish and I felt a chill go down my spine.

At that moment, right on cue, Enano dropped his flaming dumb-bells and the first of Lae Khoe's fuses caught. A fizzing noise like a hissing snake was audible as the first explosion went off. An array of fireworks shot up from the centre of the stage – a bloom of red, orange, green, white – like exploding petals. The audience screamed as fire rain fell upon them. The other acrobats flung their flaming batons down and fuse after fuse caught, succeeded by an array of explosions in every direction. Lae Khoe had truly excelled himself. There were rockets that shot to the roof then burst into buds of flame; whizzing fireflies that curled and twisted; showers of shooting stars; and the ones he called "dancing girls", which spun in screaming circles.

The result was chaos – the audience scrambling out of the stands, trampling over each other in a stampede to escape, Florenzo in the middle of the ring, calling for calm, protesting that this was part of the show, that it was all perfectly safe … to remain seated and enjoy the rest of the spectacle.

"Go!" Madame La Barboule was beside us, shoving bundles into our hands, pulling a cloak over my shoulders to disguise the wedding dress. "Quickly – while he is distracted."

She was shoving us towards the doorway. There was noise and smoke everywhere, the animals were baying and stamping in their cages, terrified by the bangs and the sulphurous smell, crowds of people were spilling out into the dark night, screaming. I could not see my father anywhere.

"Thank you," I said. "For everything."

La Barboule looked at me for a moment. "I always wanted a daughter."

"And a son?" asked Kata.

La Barboule laughed and nodded. "And a son!" Then she took each of us by the hand and looked at me. "I will look after your father." She drew our hands together. "And, you two, look after each other."

I took in her face one last time. Fireworks were going off all around her like a halo of fire, encircling her golden locks so that she looked like a siren wrapped in buds of flame.

"Now, go!"

And so Kata and I ran out into the dark night of the city.

Chapter 29

Ishmael had said that Wraithmell would find us, but as we ran through the darkened alleys of New York I wondered how he was supposed to do that – and how we would even know who he was if he did.

"La Barboule said he would use the code word," said Kata, who was doubled up under an old piece of sacking in a not very successful attempt to disguise his giant height.

"But what is the code word?"

"She didn't say."

We made our way past the custom house, through a maze of slums and down to the docks. As we neared the point where the East River meets the Hudson, the smell of salt water brought back a wave of memories of the Basin, and suddenly I felt horribly homesick. I wondered how Kata would have fitted in there – with Tommy Tucker and Jenny Stocking and the little match girl. Would he have been any safer than he was here? Or would his face, his height, his difference, always make him a target for those who seek to exploit anyone different? Are human beings cruel the world over, or might there be a place where a boy like Kata could find a home? Where I might do the same?

The docks were still crawling with life at this time of night, the sound of raucous singing pouring out of the taverns, drunken mariners staggering along the harbour, cloaked figures lingering in the shadows, trading in every form of contraband. Madame La Barboule had said to go to the quay, so we made our way under the light of a crescent moon. The sound of ships creaking and heaving on the water filled the air, a familiar chorus that made Victor pop his nose out of my pocket. When I first moved to the Basin I had been frightened of the eerie creaking at night, until my aunt told me it was the ships talking to one another. I could hear them conversing now, passing secret messages from rigging to topmast, mainsail to crow's nest. Were they passing intelligence to Wraithmell, so he knew where to find us? Or were the tall ships spies for Florenzo, who must surely have noticed our absence now?

I felt an arm on my shoulder, and then a voice spoke in a hushed whisper. "Captain Ishmael sails on the *Moby Dick* tonight."

And then we were being ushered down a set of slimy steps off the quay, down towards the inky-black water where a small rowing boat lay hidden from view in the shadow of the harbour wall.

"Do you think that was the password?" Kata asked me in a whisper.

My heart was beating double time, making Victor palpitate in my pocket. I had been unable to get a proper look at our new companion, who gestured us into the boat as he leapt expertly on board. Was his the face from the Wanted poster?

Once we were all on board, he began rowing in practised strokes that seemed to make neither splash nor sound upon the water. He kept to the shadows, to the dark slipstreams where the boat was almost invisible. Though the moon was high I could barely make out his features, but from the way he navigated the waterways I recognised him for a smuggler – a carrier of contraband, expert in evading the law.

"Are you William Wraithmell?" I whispered.

"Maybe," he said in a low voice, not looking up from

the hat that was pulled low over his face. "Sometimes."

"Thank you," I said. "For helping us."

"Ishmael is an old friend," said Wraithmell. He looked up and I could just make out his eyes – small and alert – constantly darting from side to side, constantly on watch.

"Well, for his sake and ours – thank you."

We rowed on through the night. Wraithmell never seemed to tire. I tried to work out which way we were going by the stars, but I soon became dizzy and disorientated by the myriad constellations that recalled the fireworks at the emporium.

"Do you think everyone got out safely?" I whispered to Kata.

"I hope so," he said. We were both remembering our friends at the circus. Was he thinking particularly of Mignon?

I was still wearing the antiquated wedding gown, flowers threaded through my hair on the instructions of Florenzo himself, who had insisted that I resemble Elizabeth in every point. I felt silly dressed like this, and I was cold besides. I pulled the cloak tightly round me, wanting to move closer to Kata for warmth, but something stopped me.

"Do you think it caused much damage?"

"The roof caught fire."

I turned to the low voice. It was Wraithmell who spoke, adding, "The fire crew were called to put out the blaze."

"The animals?" Kata asked in alarm.

"La Barboule will keep them safe."

The moonlight caught Wraithmell's face momentarily and I recognised his features from the poster, but even the lunar light did nothing to illuminate the man's true nature – he had a forgettable face, features you would be unlikely to remember, apart from eyes of a startling grey that met mine with an inscrutable gaze, and the scar that ran across one side of his profile. Otherwise I could not read him. He seemed opaque, almost invisible in his ordinariness – this small man who looked like a pedlar, dressed in an assortment of furs over a coarse leather jerkin and heavy mariners' boots, and who was known as Wraithmell, as Harvey Birch, Enoch Crosby or Culpepper. Why did he have so many names? How had he known Ishmael? What was his connection with the glamorous La Barboule? I had so many questions, the most of important of which was: could we trust him?

And did we have any choice?

Chapter 30

The steady motion of the oars, and the stillness of the night as we made our way from the city, soon lulled Victor to sleep. He slept more and more since our Arctic adventure. His fur had begun turning snowy white too, and he was not as speedy as he had once been.

We were slipping along dark tributaries lined with trees that curved inwards to make tunnels of branches, through which the boat passed soundlessly. Wraithmell said not a word and I felt sleep pressing upon me like a dark, winged creature, tiptoeing over my brow. I tried to fight it but eventually exhaustion overtook me.

Kata must have slept too, for we both woke to the rough scraping of the bow of the boat on shingle.

During the night I had curved myself into his body and he had wrapped himself round mine. The rough bumping lurched us apart, and I felt suddenly cold in the chill pre-dawn mist.

Wraithmell was jumping out, pulling the boat up on to a small cove hidden from the main tributary by a cunning arrangement of branches. The night was almost done – slivers of pink creeping through the raven wings of the clouds, the moon low on the horizon. How long had we slept? Where were we?

"Jump out," said Wraithmell. We did as we were told and the smuggler tugged the boat up the beach towards a fallen tree, covering it hastily with branches and dead wood so that within minutes it was completely invisible.

"Here," he said, tossing me a parcel he had retrieved from the boat. "Get dressed."

The parcel contained two sets of clothes not dissimilar to his own – one fashioned for me, one in larger proportions for Kata. He might not be a great talker but Will Wraithmell was certainly prepared.

I slipped behind a tree, took off the bridal gown and pulled on the rough, homespun clothes, transferring a still sleepy Victor to the pocket of my jerkin, another wave of last night's homesickness suddenly catching me off guard. "We are a long way from home, my friend."

Victor looked up at me and blinked dozily, his snowy-white nose giving him the appearance of an old man.

"Yes, you are right," I said, stroking his greying tail. "We don't really have a home any more. Wherever we lay our weary heads must be enough – for now."

I rolled up the wedding dress, shoved my hair up roughly into the cap Wraithmell had procured, and emerged to find that Kata and the smuggler had made a small fire on the beach and were cooking bacon. As both turned to look at me, I felt myself flushing. The expression on Kata's face was hard to make out. I had been pretty – beautiful even – for a few brief moments on stage, thanks to the ministrations of La Barboule, wreathed in flowers and attired in bridal lace. Not as beautiful as Mignon but as pretty, perhaps, as I was ever going to be. Now I was just me.

"You look like you again!" Kata smiled.

I wasn't sure how to take this, but the smell of the bacon made my stomach rumble, so I forced the crumpled wedding dress into my knapsack, took a proffered piece of bacon and a hunk of bread and devoured them hungrily.

I saved crumbs for Victor, and Wraithmell watched me feed my sleepy little friend with interest, although he made no comment.

I still had so many questions, but there was something about Wraithmell – his quiet manner, closed expression, the clothes that blended into the forest – that did not invite interrogation.

"Where are we?" was all I managed.

"Connecticut," he said, his voice low, unmodulated, hard to make out in the still morning. "Dark country – on the border between Delaware and Mohican lands."

"And where are we going?" asked Kata, who seemed more at home than I out here. Perhaps the wilderness was not so different from the snowlands – a new colour but the same vast, empty, people-less space.

"North – to Canada," said Wraithmell.

Canada seemed a long way from New York, or London. An impossible distance suddenly.

"Under US law, Kata belongs to the count," said Wraithmell, staring out at the silent waters. "In Canada you are free from the law; you can cross the Arctic Circle. Go back to your people."

"My – people?"

I thought of the Inuit – of old Ahnah, whose days were numbered by coughs that wracked her body, of Cudrun, who sold Kata to the highest bidder, of the Inuit men who had assisted in his capture. Were those really his people? And if not, who was? Kata was the

159

son of an English explorer and an outcast monster brought to life in Geneva. To whom, to where, did he truly belong?

"Or you can make a new home for yourself, as many do in the virgin territory," said Wraithmell.

"A new home?" The words seemed to open in me a gnawing ache of hunger that would not be filled with bacon and bread.

"How far is it?" asked Kata.

"Long way," said Wraithmell. "And Florenzo is probably already on our tail."

Kata looked terrified. "He is coming … for me?"

I glanced once again at my friend and remembered why we were doing this. We had to get Kata to safety and then, only then, would there be time for thoughts of the future.

"If you do everything I say, then there is no way he will find us," said Wraithmell. "If not – who knows."

Chapter 31

We travelled by night and slept by day. Once the provisions La Barboule had given us were gone, we ate berries and nuts and any living thing that Wraithmell managed to shoot or catch with the ingenious wires and traps he set up.

We followed invisible pathways through the forest. Wraithmell seemed to recognise every fallen tree, every gully, every new sapling, every trickle of fresh water. He knew where nuts and berries grew and which ones would kill us. He navigated by the stars and moon, never checking a map, never tiring, though we walked for hours without stopping. And he took care to leave no trace of our progress: we walked along streams where neither our footprints nor our scent would be traceable, and on land he used a forked stick to brush away our footsteps. Every now and then we reached another hidden cove and Wraithmell would scramble under a pile of branches to produce a dug-out that would take us further upstream. I wondered what he did when he wasn't accompanying a circus fugitive and the daughter of a ruined sea captain. What occupation required quite so many hidden boats?

For three days and nights we did not encounter another human being, nor see any signs of human habitation. Wraithmell rarely said anything, and Kata and I seemed to have forgotten how to talk to one another. We journeyed for hours, in the dark, in silence, till every part of my body hurt. I walked half asleep and grew so tired I could barely remember why were doing this.

And then on the fourth night, as dawn crept through the clouds and we made our way down a steep bank, an arrow whistled past my head, close enough that its shaft skimmed my left ear.

I ducked as another shot past. Suddenly we were all frantically scrambling down the bank to get to cover. We were exposed in a gully with our assailants somewhere above us – like shooting fish in a bowl.

"Move, move!" cried Wraithmell.

Another arrow whistled.

My foot caught on a tree branch and I felt myself rolling down the muddy bank. In my pocket Victor was emitting a series of violent squeaks. And then a rough giant hand was dragging me to safety behind a fallen tree where Kata crouched, panting with fear.

"Thank you!" I said, turning to my friend – the first words we had exchanged in what felt like days. He just nodded and seemed about to say something, but then a voice called out from the bank, and another arrow landed in the bark an inch from Kata's eye.

I gasped in horror, but Wraithmell calmly tugged out the arrow and studied it, then did something that made no sense whatsoever. He stood up and walked out into the open, his hands in the air, calling in a language I did not understand.

"What are you doing?" I hissed.

Wraithmell shouted again. I expected to see him caught by an arrow but none came. There was an answering call from above and a man appeared – a man such as I had never seen before.

"You're getting careless in your old age, William Wraithmell!"

"And you are losing your aim, Natty Bumppo, or you would have pierced my heart with one of these wasted arrows!"

"Perhaps I was not shooting to kill!" said the man, who stared down at us from high on the ridge – an old, old man who looked as though he had grown out of the very bark of the trees themselves.

"Then what are you up to, Hawkeye?" demanded Wraithmell. "Or should I call you Deerslayer? Pathfinder? Leatherstocking? What name do you go by these days?"

"I am just an old trapper now, Will – or should I call you Harvey? Either way, I am here to warn you." The old man's voice sounded almost like the cry of an ancient soothsayer. "Tom Loker is on your trail."

Chapter 32

The man, whom Wraithmell continued to call alternately Deerslayer, Leatherstocking, Hawkeye and Natty Bumppo, took us to a nearby cave, hidden by overhanging rocks. It might once have been home to one of the giant bears that Wraithmell said roamed these forests, for the cavern gave off a deep animal thrum, and long scratch marks ran criss-cross down the walls. Had the bear abandoned its home or would it come back and find us trespassers within?

It was nearly dawn, so we lit a fire, and our new companion produced a hare carcass from the bag slung round his waist and began to skin it. I was so exhausted, so hungry, I could barely keep my eyes open, and yet neither could I keep my eyes from our erstwhile assailant, to whom Wraithmell now introduced us.

"This is Natty," he said. "Though he goes by many names. Moravian born, raised by the Lenape, he is foster brother to the great Chingachgook, whom they call the last of the Mohicans, heir to the legacy of the Delaware people and all the nations of the Hudson River valley."

"For as long as the stars and the moon shall shine!" said Bumppo with a wry smile.

He looked as though he had been born of the very forest itself, and as long ago as the stars themselves first came into being – long hair spilling halfway down his back, bare-chested, his face painted with a clay mixture, torso covered in fading tattoos. His skin was leathery, as dark almost as the tree bark, but his eyes were blue, and he was so old – older than Ishmael, older than Lae Khoe, older than Ahnah … older than the forests themselves, it seemed to me.

"I didn't believe it when I heard you were smuggling human flesh, Will," he said, glancing at Kata with a look of quiet curiosity. "Why are you helping this boy?"

Wraithmell looked up sharply but said nothing. It was a question I had wanted to ask him many times, but his manner did not invite questions. Now he paused, seemingly lost in thought.

Wraithmell turned the skewer of meat over the flames, watching it drip grease as it changed from pinkish red to charred brown.

Bumppo surveyed Kata once more. He did not seem to look at him but rather around him – at something in the air that hovered in the margins that the rest of us perceived not.

"You know they say this boy wasn't created at all?" he said, his ancient voice somehow at home in this darkened bear cavern. "That he's the creation of an arrogant scientist who believed he could play god."

"That was his father," I cut in, suddenly defensive of my friend. "Kata was born like any other child. I mean … he's obviously large…"

"And he has that face!" added Bumppo, carving knife held aloft.

"Who are you to talk?" said Wraithmell. "There must be a reason you need to cover your ugly mug in all that paint!"

Bumppo looked as if he were going to punch the smuggler, but then he let out a laugh; a deep low belly chuckle that had an infectious quality, for soon we were all laughing and Wraithmell was handing round strips of cooked meat and for a moment I felt happier than I had in days.

"So what's this about Loker?" asked Wraithmell as we all chewed on the hare, which had a rich, dark, musty quality.

"Word is your Count Florenzo is none too happy about his star act absconding," said Bumppo, his long torso reflecting the dancing colours of the firelight in the gloom. "He employed Tom Loker to track him down."

"Who is Tom Loker?" I asked, licking the grease off my fingers and coaxing a reluctant Victor to manage a small morsel of meat.

"Only the most infamous slave-catcher between Mexico and the Great Lakes," said Wraithmell.

My stomach gave a lurch.

"What's he doing this far north?" Wraithmell asked Bumppo.

"He was on the tail of some runaway from Georgia, I heard. Kid got as far as Brooklyn too – hid himself away in the city, got a job in the stockyards, passed off as a freedman. Carried it off for nearly a year before Loker caught up with him. Loker cited the Fugitive Slave Law, collected his ten dollars, then shipped the slave-boy to his master."

Wraithmell whistled through his teeth. "Loker is like a dog on a scent. Can't let it go till he finds his quarry.

Might take him years but he never gives up. Never."

My stomach lurched again in quick fear. "And now he is after us?"

"Florenzo offered him a hundred-dollar reward to capture the boy – alive, mind," said Bumppo. "As for the girl—"

"My name is Maggie," I said. Victor's refusal to eat worried me, and now this Tom Loker terrified me. Would we ever be safe? Could we even trust this man who stared at Kata with such strange curiosity?

"I know who you are, Maggie Walton," said Bumppo, staring at me in the same way he had beheld Kata. "Florenzo wants you alive or dead; he don't much care neither way."

I felt a shiver go down my spine and Victor, curled up in my hand, shivered too.

"And he is already after us?"

"Reckon you got two days' lead," said the ancient woodsman. "But if I can find you, then so can Loker."

Chapter 33

Wraithmell decided we needed to move faster, and that meant taking risks, moving by day, taking routes that crossed human habitation or open plains. The going was harder than ever – more walking, more difficult terrain, more danger. But the mood was a little lighter, the atmosphere more convivial now that Natty Bumppo accompanied us.

He was certainly more of a talker than Wraithmell. Indeed he talked so much I could almost have forgotten that Victor slept more and more, and that Kata and I now barely talked at all any more. Natty claimed to have walked all the way to the Pacific Ocean, to have seen all the lands that lay from East Coast to West. Between him and our smuggler friend, they knew every inch of the surrounding territory, every trick to cover the tracks of four fugitives, one of whom with conspicuously large footprints. Wraithmell went ahead, Natty went last, disturbing leaves, grass, breaking twigs to distract the slave-catcher, Loker, whose hot breath I could almost feel down our necks. We trailed pine branches behind us, and Natty also had a jar of civet – the secretions of a wild cat that were particularly noxious to smell and which caused Victor great alarm – and he marked trees and rocks as we passed to disguise our scent.

"Loker has dogs," he said. "And a gang of trackers who know these woods better than any. He will find us – no doubt of that. But we need to get you to safety before he does."

Safety. Freedom. Home. Those three words I whispered to myself in the long days and nights. Safety. Freedom. Home. That's what we were doing this for. That's what lay at the end of this journey – if we could ever reach the end.

Natty talked to take our mind off the danger on our tail. He talked of how the ancient wilderness was being sacrificed in the name of expanding civilisation, and yet we were several days into our journey before we encountered the first human habitation in the woods. A haphazard collection of houses, carved out of a clearing, which looked as if they could be swallowed back up by the wilderness at any moment. Wraithmell told us to remain hidden while he went to purchase supplies. Kata and I crouched with Natty, watching the inhabitants of this small scrappy settlement go about their business.

"How long have people been here?" I asked.

"People have lived here since the stars and moon were created," said Natty, with an odd expression. "Just not *these* people."

"Your people?" asked Kata, who had struck up a mainly silent bond with the ancient woodsman, as if the two shared some secret kinship. They spoke often alone and if I hadn't been so tired I might almost have been jealous.

"No, I was bought up by the Lenape," Natty explained. "The Mohawk were our neighbours; they inhabited these woods for hundreds of years. I say *inhabited* not owned, for the life of man is short and the life of the hills and vales and woods is eternal – they never belong to us. We are simply granted the span of our lifetime to care for nature as it provides for us."

"What happened to those people – the Mohawk?"

"Settlers came – like these. The Mohawk made them welcome. This is a fertile valley; plenty for all to subsist on. Treaties were signed – and broken. The settlers began to mark out land for themselves, to claim ownership; they cut down trees that have stood for hundreds of years. When the Mohawk fought to protect the forest, troops came in and drove them out."

"They were driven out of their home," said Kata. His wounds were healing but his face was still criss-crossed with scars from Florenzo's beatings, bruised in an odd conglomeration of yellow and blue. But his expression was pained with a different kind of wound. He knew something of being driven out too.

"Where are they now?"

"The government in their generosity granted the Mohawk safe passage to the land they call 'Indian Territory'," said Natty with a sardonic smile. "A stretch of the poorest land east of Missouri. They were told that if they moved peacefully, they might reside there forever – or till they die out on the barren desert."

"And if they resisted?"

"They were shot."

I glanced at the little settlement. A tough weed of a place, growing up through the bare stumps of desecrated trees – pushing its way into existence. But at what cost? Kata and I were seeking freedom, safety, a new home, somewhere to settle. Was it possible to do so without causing harm to others? Must someone always be pushed out? Excluded? Was that the way the world works?

Wraithmell returned with supplies – a ham, some cornmeal, a hunk of cheese and bread – which we all fell upon hungrily.

"No news of Loker," he said.

I felt a wave of relief wash over me.

"But they asked a lot of questions, so I'm not thinking we linger here too long. These new settlers are the most suspicious, most easily riled. An' they knew I was buying food for more'n a scrappy dog like me."

"Where to now then?" I asked nervously.

"I have an idea but it's risky." Wraithmell glanced at Natty, who nodded. "If it works it gets you miles of clear blue sky between you an' Loker."

"And if it doesn't?"

Wraithmell didn't answer.

"Just east of here they're building the railroad," he said. "Folks talk of a track that will run from ocean to ocean – join the east to the west – so you can cross America in a couple of days."

Natty shook his head. "An' that will spell the end of all the nations on the Great Plains – forever."

"Right now they're building from a depot in

Shaunasee. The line stretches fifty miles east an' the man in the store says they are looking for labour to extend it another hundred by fall. Leaving in two days from now."

I glanced at Kata. We had spent no time alone since we left the emporium and I had no idea what he was thinking any more.

"We get you on that workforce and you'll be spirited fifty miles away in a matter of hours," Wraithmell continued.

Fifty miles in a few hours. It seemed impossible. And yet it would get us clear of Loker – and closer to our dream of safety, and freedom.

"On a … train?" asked Kata.

"Yup."

"It's like a sled," I tried to explain. "Only faster – and it doesn't need dogs to pull it."

In truth I had never been on a train either. Part of me was thrilled at the prospect. Fifty miles in a couple of hours, but also further from my father. Closer to safety in Canada – but was it any closer to finding a home?

"What do you think, Kata?"

Kata's eyes met mine as they had that first time on board the ship when I had cleaned his wound. My heart jumped in my chest. It was the first time he had looked at me properly for days, and in his eyes I saw that Kata still trusted me with his life. And I knew I had to do whatever it took to keep him safe. I could not betray that trust.

I glanced at the settlement in the woods. These people had found a place, made a home. Could Kata and I do the same?

I turned to Wraithmell. "Will it work?"

He turned to me and said simply, "Only if we get there before Loker."

Chapter 34

The town of Shaunasee was very different to the settlement in the woods. The canals had brought commerce this way several decades since, and now the development of the new railway had transformed a small mining community surviving on the salt pans into a bustling new metropolis – not yet rivalling New York, but with big ambitions.

Stepping into plain sight after so many days in the wilderness was terrifying – and we were to do it alone. Natty would not venture near the outskirts of the town, and Wraithmell was too well known by the authorities to risk accompanying us beyond the railway depot. From there on we would be on our own, just Kata and me. Could we do it alone? Did we have any choice?

"I like the company of trees more than people," Bumppo said as he parted from us. "I'll watch out for Loker, head him off if I can. Buy you a little time."

"Thank you," I said. For a man who claimed not to like people, Natty Bumppo was perhaps the most human man I had ever met, and I lamented the fact that our journey seemed to be full of goodbyes. Every time we encountered people with good hearts and kind souls we were forced to part from them.

"It has been my pleasure to serve the boy with the rainbow soul," said Bumppo, with a small bow in Kata's direction.

I looked up in surprise. "What did you call him?"

The ancient man smiled. We were standing in a clearing through which the sunshine fell in dappled shafts. "Each man is really a spirit – an *atiq* – encased in a bodily shell," he said. "Most folks stare so hard at the shell they fail to see the colours of the soul."

"What does a person's soul look like?"

The sun shone through the canopy on to Natty and the air seemed to hum with the promise of springtime as he spoke. "Yours, Maggie Walton, is blue like the sea when the sun shines upon it– many flickering colours from turquoise to deepest ink, rippling, never still, but beautiful, always full of strength."

I caught my breath for a moment. Nobody had ever called me beautiful before. Nor strong. I thought for a moment of Kata's mother – she had been beautiful and strong. Was it possible that I could one day be like her?

"Will here is the colour of fall leaves trodden in the mud," Natty went on. "Flickers of gold – earthy, mulchy. Hard to read."

Wraithmell laughed.

"And Kata?"

Natty stared hard, yet not at Kata – around him, through him – as I had seen him do before. "I see all the colours of the Northern Lights – and yet it is as white as lightning too, as white as snow, as white as pearl – all the many hues of white, more than I knew existed. I have never seen such a spirit before. Wherever there are people who see men by the colour of their souls, and not the colour of their skin or the shape of their features – there you will be welcomed, cared for, kept safe."

My heart leapt in my chest. "But how will we know who they are?"

Natty turned to me now. I was aware of every sound of the forest, of the low thrumming of the sunlight, the sigh of the trees, the call of birds. "Look for the light they cast in the world. Close your eyes and look with your inner sight."

I stared really hard at him then – tried to visualise any colours floating around him, but although the sounds and colours of the forest seemed to take on a brighter, sharper hue, I could see nothing.

"It takes time." Bumppo placed an ancient palm on my shoulder and smiled. "But don't stop looking, Maggie Walton. Never stop looking."

Chapter 35

It was strange to be back in human habitation after so long in the wilderness. The town seemed dirty and cheap and tawdry after the simple majesty of the forest: the dime stores and saloons and warehouses; the wagons rolling along the rutted tracks. The competing sounds and sights and smells of town life assaulted my senses and made me feel nervous, exposed. Wraithmell had said it was as easy to stay hidden in a town as in the forest, particularly a frontier town filled with all species of human kind: chancers and runaways and desperate men. And yet I felt as I had in the gully – like a fish in a bowl, target practice, easy prey.

As we walked down the bustling main street towards the railway depot, I felt as if everyone was looking at us, as if we might encounter Tom Loker round every corner. I saw advertising posters tacked up everywhere. "Indian Land for Sale – A Home of your Own in the Fine Lands of the West!" read one. "California – Cornucopia of the World – 43,000 Acres of Government Land Untaken," said another. "750,000 acres of Indian Land Open to Settlers – Register Now!" declared a third.

I began to relax a little as we walked on. The town was so full of every kind of person, they barely looked askance at a trio made up of a giant boy with an asymmetrical face, a muddy-faced girl dressed as a boy, and a slouch-shouldered trapper with his hat pulled so low you couldn't make out the face that featured on Wanted posters the length and breadth of New York state.

"I won't go in with you," said Wraithmell, once we reached the railway depot. "But I'll be here. You won't see me, but I'll stay till you depart."

"Will," I asked, "where do we go after the railroad?"

"Well now, there's more than one kind of railroad in America."

"What does that mean?"

But William Wraithmell, inscrutable as ever, had already turned to cross the road. He was about to leave us, and I had no idea where were supposed to go next. We had no map, no new contact to look out for, no idea where we were really going.

"What railroad?" I cried out. "What do you mean?"

But he was on the other side of the road. A cart full of manure went past, and a gaggle of laughing women dressed in striped poplin. Wraithmell was there one minute and then he was gone, disappearing as unobtrusively as he had first appeared, melting into the crowds as if he had never been.

Without another word. Without even saying goodbye.

Now Kata and I were on our own. I turned to my tall friend and took a deep breath, then pushed open the door of the railway depot. The foreman sat behind a large desk ingeniously constructed out of old beer barrels and railway sleepers – a portly, flame-haired man who reminded me of the red-haired Scotsman on the *Moby Dick*. I wondered if the railroads were for some what the sea was for mariners – a chance to sail into unchartered territory.

"We want to sign up," I said, trying to sound more confident than I felt, as I indicated the poster on the wall that offered "Wild Wild West Careers for Hard-working Men – Wages $1 a day! Apply to H. O'Malley, Agent, the Mohawk and Kilkanney

Railroad Company Inc."

The man – whom I took to be agent H. O'Malley – looked us up and down, chewing on a ball of tobacco that rolled around his mouth, the dark sticky paste visible with every mastication, his ginger whiskers quivering. I stuck my chin up and hoped he would not see my trembling hands.

"Your man there looks strong enough, to be sure," he said, in an accent I recognised from the Basin as Irish.

"Has he got any brains, though?" he asked, whiskers a-quiver. "Does the man machine talk, or what?"

I didn't like the way this man spoke about Kata, rather than to him. I pushed away my nerves and spoke for him. "He talks three languages, actually. And he can do the work of three men."

O'Malley looked at me, the sticky black tobacco rolling round and round on his tongue. "An' you've got enough talk for three of him, to be sure. But what'll we be wanting with a scrap of a thing like you? I don't pay for the chat!"

"I'm stronger than I look," I said, pulling myself up as tall as I could.

"That don't say much," he said, with a tobacco-sticky laugh. His teeth were blackened with the gum residue but his eyes were a bright, vivid green and not unkind. "An' that English accent won't win you no friends in these parts, God knows. Where you from, *boy*?" He pronounced the last word with a hint of sarcasm.

"Shadwell Basin," I said.

"London Town! And the giant?"

Kata still seemed to be struck mute.

"He's from Baffin Island," I said.

"Well, you're an odd couple, an' no mistake." He looked us up and down, trying to figure out a sum that didn't quite add up.

"But a couple is what we are," I said defiantly, determined not to be bested by this ginger-whiskered bully. "You want the man machine, you get me too."

"Yes," said Kata. "We are a pair."

I looked up at him and smiled in gratitude. I wondered how he felt seeing the tables turned. In this world I was worthless, while his strength and size counted for something. Nobody cared what you looked like here, so long as you could dig a trench, hew stone and haul sleepers from dawn till dusk.

Kata smiled back at me. It felt like the first smile in a long, long time.

"Is that so?" said O'Malley. "Well, sign here. We

leave at sunrise, so say goodbye to your sweethearts and be at the depot 6 a.m. sharp. You belong to the railroad now."

Chapter 36

It was already late afternoon. We had just a few hours left of daylight and the night to kill before the train departed, carrying us far away to safety on the Great Plains, away from the reach of Loker, of Florenzo. I wanted to lay low, stay out of sight, but for Kata the town held so many novelties. He had grown up in the snowlands – all he had known was the cave, the village, then the ship, then the circus, and the woods. Apart from our brief flight across New York and the cabin in the forest, he had never seen a human settlement not made of ice and snow.

"Can we look?" he asked, gazing towards the general store and the saloon from which music floated into the soft late-afternoon air.

I glanced around nervously. We still had no idea how close Loker was but the chance to see Kata smile again was so tempting – and maybe there was no harm. After all, Wraithmell had said you could lose yourself in a town as easily as the woods.

"Come on," I said. "But don't draw attention to yourself."

It was a foolish thing to say. This might be a town where all manner of mankind might pass unnoticed, even Kata – a boy who stood at six foot eight in his bare feet. But what made him conspicuous was the way he marvelled at the array of items in the store – it didn't exactly mark him out as a regular. He picked up a tin of beans and stared. Then his brow furrowed at the sight of a pair of spectacles, before his face lit up at a small tin whistle.

"Kata, don't…"

But he had already put it to his lips.

The woman behind the counter looked up sternly, but then her face changed.

"Why, he looks mighty different but he ain't nobbut a lad, is he?" she said. She was a mousy-haired lady, maybe forty years old, in a striped poplin dress with starched cap and lace shawl. She spoke in a voice as mousy as her hair, but her pale-green eyes misted as they fixed on Kata.

"I had a boy once," she said with a gentle smile on her lips.

She emitted a sigh. Kata had put down the whistle and was listening. Even Victor had woken from his long slumber and poked out his snowy-white old-mouse nose to see what was going on.

"My boy never grew quite like the other children; his limbs ditn't work for a long time," the dime-store lady went on in her soft wispy tones. "Spoke late an' walked later – an' then he was always falling over – over his feet, over his words. But he was good as gold. As kind an' sweet a boy as you ever knew."

"What happened to him?" I asked. I dared not linger here for too long but her story somehow held us both in thrall.

"Oh, well, he ditn't' live past his twelfth birthday." There was a slight quaver in her voice. "I always knew he warn't long for this world."

Victor's bright little eyes were fixed on the mousy-haired lady and he gave a little sigh, as if the world her long-lost boy belonged to quivered every day closer in his dreams. I felt tears spring involuntarily to my eyes as I thought of my own mother, of Aunt Maggie, or Kata's mother – and of all the others to whom we had bid farewell.

"Folks looked at my boy askance," said the store-mistress. "Said he should be locked up, put away out of sight of God-fearing folks. But he warn't but a child."

Kata reached out to return the tin whistle. "You keep it, boy!" she said. "I can't give my baby no more gifts – an' for all you are so big and your face so mussed up, you remind me of him. You keep it!"

We made our way out of the store and down the main street. Kata and I were more at ease with each other than we had been for weeks. I pointed out the post office and explained to Kata how you could write to someone anywhere in the world. Then we passed the saloon where withered-looking, and mean-looking, and lost-looking men all sat drinking whisky and chewing tobacco on the porch.

It was sliding into evening now and my fears about Loker grew with every hour that passed. So we slipped down to the railway depot where the great locomotive stood idle like an ancient beast, waiting to be reawakened in a billow of steam and belching flame in the morning. Kata stared as I looked around for somewhere we could sleep without being detected.

"How does it move?"

"Something to do with coal and steam – and pistons."

My father had explained it to me once. My father, who knew so much about so many things and who was now a punchbag popcorn-seller in a New York circus. Whom I hadn't even said goodbye to.

I managed to find an unlocked door on one of the freight trucks and we squeezed among barrels of black dust, like that which Lae Khoe had used on the night of our escape.

"Don't light a match in here," I told Kata. "We'll go up like one of Lae Khoe's Roman candles!"

The dynamite would be good for disguising our scent, but I used some of Natty's civet too, daubing it on the doorway in case our would-be captors arrived before the train's departure. William Wraithmell had trained us well but Loker would not be far behind us; every hour we stayed here brought him closer. I could hardly wait for sunrise.

"No matter how good a tracker Loker is, he can hardly compete with the speed of a train, can he, my little mouseling!"

I was sitting by the carriage doorway, trying to stay awake. Kata was fast asleep. The sky outside was full of stars and the town was swaddled in pre-dawn hush. Victor was awake for once, perched on my knee, watching as I scribbled a letter to Madame La Barboule on a piece of paper she had given me for the purpose when we left the circus. I wanted my father to know that we were safe, that we would find a place to settle, and that then I would come back for him. I would free him too.

"How are you feeling, Victor?" I asked, running a finger down the snowy-white fur of his back and noting the prominence of his ribs beneath. I hadn't been able to coax him to eat for days and his breath seemed shallower than normal tonight. "Was the Arctic too much for you? Maybe I should never have taken you – but I could hardly bear to have left you behind."

Victor squeaked in agreement and nuzzled his nose against my finger.

"I won't ever leave you behind. You know that, don't you?"

I was thinking of my father, of all the times he had sailed away and left me bereft. The same thing Kata's father had done. And his father before him. A pattern of abandonment stretching back across the generations.

"Who are you writing to?"

For a second I thought Victor had spoken – that my little mouseling, who had been my only real friend for so long, had finally found a way to say in words what he had communicated so long with his eyes. But I turned to see that Kata was awake in the darkness. The deep, star-filled hush of the night seemed to cocoon us; nothing could touch the three of us in that moment.

"I am writing to La Barboule," I said. "She told me of a place I could address the letters to – a milliner's shop – so that Florenzo could not intercept them. You could write to Mignon if you wanted."

I stared out at the stars as I said the last bit, to avoid looking him in the face.

"And to my father?"

I looked round.

"You said at the post office that you can write a letter to anywhere in the world. Could I send one to my father?"

In the darkness I could only just make out his features. The gloaming had smoothed them out so that I could see the boy he would have been, had nature dealt him a gentler hand. His eyes were large and enquiring, his forehead smooth, his lips soft. And he looked so hopeful that I couldn't bear to crush him.

"You could, if you knew where to address the letter. If you knew he was even—"

"My father is alive!"

"I wasn't saying he wasn't. But with no address…"

I wanted to say something to make it better but I

could think of nothing. It had been a long time since it was just the three of us – since those endless ocean days when we had been so easy together. Something had changed since then, and I didn't know how to find my way back.

Kata shifted over the carriage till he was seated across from me. Victor shuffled between us, looking from one to the other, as if trying to bridge some invisible gap, as he had when my father had locked me out of the cage.

"The US mail isn't the only way of getting a message to someone," said Kata.

"What do you mean?"

"Natty said the Great Nations spread from the tip of South America to the Arctic North. That news spreads on the winds over the whole land."

"He said it used to," I said, knowing what he was thinking and the hopes he was pinning on it.

"My father will hear of me," said Kata, his eyes fixed now on the stars in the night sky. "He will come for me."

I said nothing. I knew enough of the hope that is like oxygen to men's souls. I had seen my father stripped of it, seen him reduced to a hopeless shell of a man. I could not bear that to happen to Kata. And yet was I just as naive? I was journeying to find a place

194

whose existence I could be not be sure of, some place of safety, of freedom, that might be nothing more than a dream. Like my father's dream of the monster and the promise of salvation it held.

Victor looked from one of us to the other; he seemed to be thinking the same thing. His soft white fur glowed in the starlight so that he almost seemed to twinkle.

"Yes," I said finally. "Your father will hear of you."

Chapter 37

Eventually Kata fell back to sleep. I did my best to stay awake, watching as the first tinges of pink crossed the sky, the moon lowering over the distant horizon.

Just before sunrise the depot began to stir, and labourers appeared for the great railway adventure: pale-faced Bohemians; red-haired Irish men; former slaves with the shadows of the plantations in their eyes; a group of Chinese labourers; and a couple of men with features of the Mohawk but close-cropped hair and white man's clothes. Then there was O'Malley giving out orders, the engineer waving red-faced, and the prospector – a smart-looking man in a dinner suit with a servant carrying his luggage – boarding the well-appointed carriage at the rear.

The engine was coming alive too. I could see a small boy running to and from the coal and water, stoking the giant furnace that powered the pistons, and I recalled the picture my father had drawn of the combustion system, when his brain had been filled with things other than the monster. I nudged Kata awake. The other labourers were boarding the train. My plan was to jump out of the freight truck in which we were hiding and join them at the very last minute, keeping out of sight until a few moments before departure.

But at that moment I heard men yelling, doors slamming, and a familiar voice sent a bolt of pure fear running through my body.

"Florenzo!"

Kata was immediately alert. I pushed him back into the shadows of the carriage, my heart hammering, and peered out of a crack in the doorway.

I could see a knot of people outside the depot office – O'Malley arguing with a cruel-looking man, six foot tall, one ear missing and a burn down the side of his face. He had a giant dog straining at its leash, panting as if it had caught hold of a scent and was baying to bring down its quarry.

With a leap of horror I recalled that we were its

quarry. And this was Tom Loker.

For there stood the all-too-familiar figure of Count Florenzo. No longer in his ringmaster attire, but somehow still immaculate in riding dress – as if the dust that clung to everything else hereabouts did not attach itself to him – he stood a little back from the fray, twirling his cane and surveying the crowd as if they were an audience at the circus.

"We're lookin' for a girl an' a monster!" Loker was saying. "Reward for't captoor of either."

Loker was waving a Wanted poster with our images upon it. Though the slave-catcher claimed to be looking for a girl, it would not be hard for O'Malley to recognise the pair of us, nor the lady at the dime store, nor any of the men in the saloon who had come out to see what the commotion was about. My heart was pounding in my chest. One of the tobacco-chewing men was about to speak. O'Malley stopped him. "Who's looking for 'em?"

Florenzo took a step forward, as if he were bathed in an invisible spotlight. "My name is Count Florenzo. This creature is my property."

I glanced at Kata, who blanched at the word "property".

"And the little lady? She your property too?"

"She 'elped t' foogitive escape," said Loker – his voice like the low growl of his dog, which was snarling angrily, chops dripping with saliva.

"A little girl like that," said O'Malley. "You been outwitted by a child?"

Loker's face contorted into a snarl. "Tom Loker ain't outwitted by anyone. I'm t' best slave-catcher in all America. I alwus get my man – or my gal!"

"Why don't you stick to catching slaves," said the dime-store lady. "An' quit mithering young kids."

"Slaves, runaway wives – I ain't choosy. I won't stop till I got my man," Loker said, taking a step towards the dime-store owner. "Or woo-man neither."

"Well, speaking for myself, I ain't seen no one of that description pass through here." O'Malley waved a hand dismissively at the Wanted poster. "An' your boy there would be hard to miss, sure enough."

I was desperately trying to think what to do. Florenzo was eyeing O'Malley with suspicion, then glancing around the assembled company with eagle eyes. The dime-store lady stood flushed but with her chin up, lips set. O'Malley rolled the ball of tobacco round his mouth like cud. At any moment I expected someone to speak up, but it seemed that O'Malley exerted an influence in this town that none was prepared to defy.

For while he remained silent, so did every other man, woman and child. I held my breath.

Florenzo turned in a slow circle in his invisible spotlight. In my pocket I felt Victor squirm, my own heart beating so loudly I felt sure it would give us away.

"You satisfied?" demanded O'Malley. "Cos we got a locomotive to get going, an' that's a fact!"

The engine emitted a loud billow of smoke that caused many of the assembled company to cough. Next to me I could feel Kata trembling.

"You won't mind if I gets my hound to check afore you go!" said Loker. "Just to be sure."

My heart lurched in my chest. O'Malley shrugged. "Search all you like. But this train is leaving, an' the railroad waits for no man."

Chapter 38

The giant hound was foaming at the mouth. Loker held a scrap of material to its muzzle – I recognised it as Kata's shirt from the emporium act. I felt angry and terrified and desperate all at once.

"Fetch!" commanded Loker.

And then the creature was bounding hungrily across the dusty ground towards the train. Men were clambering aboard amid shouted instructions, steam billowing from the engine, supplies being loaded. I heard O'Malley yell to the driver; heard the depot guard blow his whistle.

I could only hope the civet would confuse the beast long enough for us to get away. I saw the giant dog run round in confused circles, but then it picked up our scent and was barking excitedly, racing towards the truck where we were hidden.

"I knew they were here!" cried Florenzo with a crazed delight.

"Kata – get back!"

The engine was beginning to move – painfully slowly. I felt the wooden boards creaking beneath us as I tried to tug the door shut. It seemed stuck on its track and would not budge. Panic filed my brain. The dog was on the scent, confused by the civet, which was slowing his progress, but unmistakably heading towards the very truck where we were hiding. Loker and Florenzo were following – hunger on the face of one, something less human on the other. The carriage was moving faster now, but the dog was leaping up at the opening of the car. I flung myself into the far corner but its giant fangs were snapping, snarling at the gap in the doorway.

And then something was happening. The dog stopped leaping. The train was still moving. Instinctively I felt in my pocket.

Victor was gone.

Chapter 39

"Victor!"

I was up and at the doorway, no longer caring that Florenzo could see me, nor Loker. The engine was gaining momentum but the giant beast was no longer pursuing us – it was bounding after something on the ground, something barely visible that caused it to run around in circles, distracted by a chase that was not at the command of its master but at the call of the wild.

"Victor!"

Florenzo was screaming, "Stop the train! Get them!"

Loker was shouting at the dog but the beast was ignoring him still, caught in its chase. The train was moving at pace now and steam was billowing. The giant dog was still running in rings, zigzagging across the dust, all thoughts of me and Kata forgotten. As I watched its circles I swear, just for a second, that amid the billows of dust and steam I saw a flash of snowy white and two tiny bright eyes stop and look back at me. My heart shattered.

And then the dog pounced. And it was all over.

Chapter 40

I don't recall much of the train journey. It was fast and loud, and I was glad of both, for the speed and sound combined to fill my brain and obliterate some fraction of the pain that pounded within. I remember the country we raced across was red – the same flash of colour that had been the last I saw of my mouseling friend. Waving red grass, red earth, red sky, the dust rising up in scarlet clouds as we passed.

"He was old," said Kata, his arm round me.

"I know."

He didn't need to tell me that Victor had already far outlived his mouse years, that his fur had turned snowy white and that since the Arctic his eyes were dimmer, his movements slower, his appetite all but gone. I knew all that. But it didn't make it any better. Not even Kata's strong arms could numb the pain.

"He knew his days were numbered," I said, staring out at the sea of waving red grasses filled with giant sunflowers, some of them as tall as trees.

"He saved our lives."

"I know."

Victor had saved us, secured our freedom – but what was freedom worth without love, without companionship? I fixed my eyes on the empty red expanse of the prairie, scarlet and gold, spreading all the way out to the horizon, and said no more.

It was nearly evening when the attack happened. I must have found relief in sleep for I woke to a terrible lurch and a shattering of wood splintering against metal, cries rending the air, hooves thundering, as if the pain in my head had come alive in the sound and colour and chaos all around.

And then the world was turning upside down, my head crashing against wood, barrels flying, limbs colliding with inanimate objects, Kata leaping with an almost superhuman speed to wrap himself round me as the car lurched, toppled, tumbling off the tracks. A girder narrowly missed my head and caught Kata's instead, a blow that would have knocked any other boy unconscious but which glanced off him easily.

"What's happening?"

The carriage had come to a stop but the cries continued. Then the shattered door of the car was wrenched open and for a second, framed in the doorway, surrounded by waving red grasses like tongues of flame, I saw a figure, hair flying in the wind, bathed in a glow like sunset. Then I felt the sting as a dart hit my arm, and I turned to see that Kata had also been hit, for his face lit up in surprise then drooped, and I felt my own doing the same, and then a curtain came down in my head.

And that is the last I remember.

Chapter 41

I awoke to find myself on horseback, my body arched across the torso of an unknown rider, galloping through the waving red grasses, faster than the train, faster than the sleigh, faster than the wind itself across the ocean – or so it felt. I remembered that first journey in the snowlands – the feeling that I would miss a place for the rest of my life. I had been awake just a few seconds, aware of my new surroundings for barely time to take a breath, my heart bruised and bleeding – and yet I experienced it again.

The light was bleeding out of the sky in ruby streaks, making the red grasses glow scarlet, amber and blood red. The air was warm and sweet, the musky tang of the rider whose back I was moulded to mingling with the delicate scents of the heat and rising sap of summer. And the whole world seemed filled with the hum of inaudible music, a thousand twanging instruments humming around my ears, my soul – the music of the earth, of the spheres.

Groggy and confused, I took in the other riders alongside us – four horses in total, all galloping in beautiful unison, the long black hair of the riders flying, their bodies at one with the beasts, with the landscape.

Kata?

I experienced a start of fear.

Where was Kata?

I saw him then, slung over the back of another rider, almost as tall as himself. His head lolled sleepily, as I felt my own doing. Relief swept over me. The idea of losing Kata as well as Victor was too much to bear. I fought against the tide of sleep that tugged at me – I needed to stay awake, to keep us safe – but oblivion tugged at me and as I drifted back into unconsciousness my final thought was: who were these people, and where were they taking us – to freedom, or the opposite?

We rode all night and all the next day without stopping, but whatever my captors had shot into me did its work well, for I drifted in and out of consciousness, sometimes dreaming we were on a ship sailing through a waving red sea, or that we were racing through blood-red snow. I woke sometimes to see Kata slung on the back of the tallest of the riders, on the horse that ran astride ours, before slipping back into ruby dreams through which wild horses and long-haired riders danced and sped.

I was starting to come round as the sun fell again. We came to a stop by a small stream, and the riders dismounted. I needed to figure out who our captors were. I had no idea which people inhabited this stretch of prairie land – their appearance was different from Natty's. There were two young men, plus a girl and a statuesque woman who had been my riding companion – apparently the leader of the small raiding party. She wordlessly assisted me from the horse but made no attempt to restrain me. Not that she had any need, for my legs buckled beneath me as they touched the dusty earth, and I couldn't have escaped even if I had wanted to. And yet for some reason, I had no desire to run. Perhaps it was the residue of the sleeping draught, perhaps grief for Victor; I had no reason to trust these people and yet instinctively I was not scared.

Kata seemed to feel the same way. He was coming round too and we sat groggily under a tree, watching our companions busy themselves making a fire, boiling water, preparing food to eat. They spoke easily to one another in their own language but did not address us.

"Who are they?" I whispered. "What do they want with us?"

"They knew we were on the train." Kata seemed a little more awake than me, and he was watching them intently.

"They must have put something on the line to derail it. But why? Are they working with Loker?"

"I don't know." Kata turned to look at me. The sunset was bleeding into red grass, haloing the scene in an eerie ruby glow. "Maggie ... about Victor—"

"Don't!" Victor's place in my pocket pulsed with the pain of my near-breaking heart.

Kata reached out his hand and wrapped his large fingers round mine. I felt the empty place in my chest throb. But I did not pull away.

I had no idea what we were supposed to do. We watched our captors prepare food – a maize porridge flavoured with strips of dried meat. They bought us some in small wooden bowls and I realised I was starving. The meat was musty and chewy but not unpleasant, and the porridge warmed me from within.

Apart from the tall woman, who was clearly the leader of the group, there did not seem to be any distinction between the younger men and the girl.

The three younger ones spoke a great deal and there was much laughter among them. The woman leader was more subdued. She ate her food in silence, occasionally glancing over to Kata and me. I kept expecting her to address us, but she never did.

"We could run away," I whispered when our captors were rolling out rush mats, preparing to sleep. The night sky filled with myriad stars and I felt sure my feet were steady enough to carry me now. "We could steal their horses and flee."

"Where to?" Kata whispered back.

He was right. We had no idea where we were. And I recalled what Natty had said about the changeable climate on the prairies: how the snow and ice came in without warning, any time of year, summer or winter; how terrible floods washed away whole settlements in mere hours; how blistering heat could burn off a man's nose and ears, peel the skin from his body; how sometimes these extremes came one on top of the other. This strange landscape stretched identically in every direction. My heart sank. Even if we could run, where were we to go?

"I don't think they work for Loker." I glanced at the leader, who sat alert, staring out into the empty black of the prairies. She was not pretty exactly, nor beautiful. One might have called her striking, her features chiselled like a sculpture out of the sandstone of her face. She looked stern, uncompromising, but I had seen evil in men's eyes and I saw none in hers. Did that mean we could trust her?

"So what do they want with us?" said Kata.

"I suppose we will have to wait and see," I said. "For now!"

Chapter 42

For a long time sleep eluded me. I knew I should be coming up with a plan to escape but all I could think of was the emptiness in my pocket. Whenever I closed my eyes I saw it all over again – the giant dog; Victor scuttling across the floor of the train car; the flash of red in the dust...

Eventually I slept – a deep, dreamless sleep under the canopy of the stars in the dark prairie night. I awoke at dawn to find our companions striking camp. Once again we were fed on the mixture of porridge and dried meat, and then we remounted the horses and set off once more. Still my rider companion and I exchanged not a word. I had no idea what she was thinking – no idea if she was taking us closer to freedom, safety. I

214

only knew that I was not afraid of her. And until I could come up with a plan of escape, that was all I had to hang on to.

We rode for several hours through a landscape that changed very little. The grasses shifted sometimes from ruby to gold to moss green then back to red again. Small copses of trees, or rocky outcrops, were all that broke the monotony of this bare, empty expanse. The sun was high in the sky when I saw the first sign of human habitation – a homestead, white-painted wooden walls, red roof, barn, wind pump, white-picket fence and a small crop of waving corn. It looked like a child's toy farm. I felt a jolt of excitement, followed quickly by fear. What was this place?

A wave of my companion's hand brought the party to a stop by a clump of trees some distance from the dwelling. There we waited, none of our party speaking or moving. All watching for something.

The air was still and unmoving. The noise of a curlew wheeling above, the horses panting hotly and my own heart hammering in my chest were the only sounds that broke the silence.

What were we waiting for?

A cry went up from Kata's rider – like the curlew's call, but with a final trill that rose higher and longer than the bird's. Cupping a hand to the lips, the sound was repeated.

And then silence.

A few minutes later we saw a figure come out of the homestead and begin to hang washing on a line strung across the yard. An old woman – white-haired, small and plump but erect in carriage, her bearing like that of a much younger lady. In a poplin dress and starched apron, she reminded me of Aunt Maggie. She hung up a sheet, an apron, then a brightly coloured quilt in a design that looked like the sun and the moon. My companion conferred with the others before lifting me off the horse and indicating that I should mount the horse carrying Kata.

Part of me wanted to turn and run as we watched her ride up to the house, stop outside the picket fence and address the old lady. I saw the woman look off into the distance. I wondered how we must appear. What did she see – friend or foe? And which was she?

I glanced at Kata, who looked as nervous as I was. Then there was another bird-like call trilling high on the air. My new companion put hands to lips and gave an answering call. And then we were all on the move, galloping out of the shelter of the trees towards the homestead.

What was happening?

We rode round the back of the house to the barn, where we quickly dismounted, the horses were tethered, and the barn doors swung open to let us inside. Every fibre of my being wanted to turn and run, but there was nowhere to run to, nothing to do but obey.

As I was shoved roughly into the dark interior, it took a few seconds for my eyes to adjust to the gloom and to realise that we were not alone. Half a dozen pairs of eyes stared up at us – bright, questioning … fearful.

Chapter 43

"This is a depot on ze underground railroad," said the plump, white-haired lady, handing out freshly baked cornbread. It was still warm and the aroma so strongly evoked Aunt Maggie baking in the kitchen at home that it made me want to cry.

After the initial terror of being thrown into the dark, I was struggling to adjust to the realisation that we were safe and with people who wanted to keep us that way.

"Underground railroad?"

I suddenly remembered that William Wraithmell had said that there was more than one kind of railroad, but I hadn't understood what he meant – and I still wasn't sure now.

"A network of safe houses," explained our hostess in soft tones that had a hint of the Old World. "To help escaping slaves. It stretches from the south all ze way up to the Canadian border."

"It's like a patchwork of kindness running across America."

This came from a voice in the darkness – the owner of one of the pairs of eyes that had greeted us. Now I saw this particular pair were set in the disarmingly beautiful face of a man with high cheekbones and a smile that illuminated the shadowy barn.

"It's made up of scraps of people who don't hold wit' slavery; don't think one man has any right to own another," he said. "Think every man – an' woman – has a right to be free."

"Free?" I felt myself flushing under the scrutiny of those eyes, that smile. "What does the railroad do? Where does it go?"

"We help slaves to escape – cross ze border to Canada where slavery is not legal," the old lady explained. "You are ze passengers – ze 'cargo'. Zere are hiding places known as stations, and stationmasters, like me, who hide slaves in zeir homes."

"They got secret signals, whistles, songs," said the owner of the illuminating smile. "Some folks puts out messages on quilts they hang on their lines."

I remembered the quilt with the elaborate pattern of suns and moons. Had that been a signal – a coded message of threads and patches? Had our captors actually been trying to save us?

"So can we ride on this railroad?" asked Kata, speaking for the first time. The rest of the group were all staring at him, taking in his giant frame.

"My husband is a conductor," our hostess continued. "He accompanies groups on ze next stage of zeir journey. Tomorrow he will take zese people to the lake where – God willing – zey will take the final steps to freedom. As will you, should you wish to do so."

Now my eyes had become accustomed to the gloom of the barn I could see the group ranged in age from a babe in arms to a grandfather, stooped and grey. They all had a look in their eyes that I had seen in Kata's – memories of pain, of fear – yet in each it was mixed in some measure with a softer more fragile light: the flicker of hope.

"I still don't understand…"

The leader of our rescue party spoke then in her own tongue.

The old lady translated for her. "Winona wishes me to tell you zat she and her people are Oglala Lakota of

Little Hawk's band. Zey intercepted ze train to bring you to safety here."

I looked at Winona and the rest of the hunting party, crouched on their haunches, chewing on the cornbread, relaxed but not fully at ease.

"How did she know we were on the train?"

Without waiting for the old lady to translate, Winona responded in her own tongue.

"She says zey heard of ze flight of ze boy with ze rainbow soul," our hostess conveyed to us.

I remembered what Kata had said on the train. Did the winds still blow across the Great Nations? Might the news really reach his father, if he were still alive?

"Please tell Winona and her people we are very grateful."

Winona nodded solemnly and said something to the other riders, who smiled and nodded also.

"Zey will incur much displeasure from ze railroad company for derailing ze train," said the old lady. "Zere will be reprisals upon zeir people. Zey took a big risk for you."

"And so do you," said the beautiful young man with the large, feeling eyes.

"Can I … can I ask your name?" I said.

"Krajek," she said. "My name is Antonia Krajek."

Chapter 44

We spent the night in the barn with our new companions. We were safe here, for now at least. There was a family from a plantation in Georgia – father, wife and two young children (their elder brother and two sisters had been sold and their father refused to allow the same to happen to his remaining offspring); a lone runaway from Alabama (the young man with the beautiful face and velvet eyes); an old man from Virginia; and three girls from Mississippi who had been sold to a camp of soldiers and escaped by turning a keg of gunpowder on their captors. They told us stories of cruel slave-owners, of being chained by the neck in the blazing cotton fields, of families separated and sold off like livestock, of slave auctions and starvation and endless servitude.

Their stories of escape were far more dangerous than ours – hiding neck-deep in swamps for days on end, being pursued by vigilantes, near starvation, exposure, and constant, constant terror.

"But now we are so close," said the young man from Alabama, whose name was Simeon. "Just a few miles to the lake, then across the water to Canada, where no one can touch us."

"And we can come with you?" It seemed too good to be true. Could the destination we had dreamed of really be so close – just a few miles away?

Mrs Krajek was to speak to her husband. The next day's departure was all arranged – the boat ready, the numbers known, the watch set. But the addition of two more to the party – particularly one as large as Kata – would complicate matters, said Mr Krajek when he returned. Was the vessel big enough? Would it place the rest of the party in danger?

I turned to Mrs Krajek in desperation. What could we say to persuade him to take us?

"Tom Loker is after zem."

"Loker?" said Mrs Krajek's husband, a leather-skinned farmer with thinning white hair and blue eyes. "We don't vant slave-catchers sniffing around zis place, putting ze whole railroad in jeopardy."

"Exactly," said his wife. "Which is why you must take zese two. Get zem away as soon as possible, and all traces of zem too."

I was so grateful to the old lady at that moment I could have hugged her. Mr Krajek turned to look at us with his old blue eyes. "Very well. Ve leave tomorrow!"

Chapter 45

The lake was not like the ocean. Flatter, stiller, as silent as a millpond, it spoke in softly lapping tongues of freedoms beyond the waves, and servitude behind. On the beach where we clambered aboard the boat in the pre-dawn gloaming we were in America – "land of the free", but only for those with white skin and regular proportions, those without a bounty on their head, I thought to myself. But on the shores mistily visible beneath the distant mountains was Canada – a new world, where ownership of human flesh was a sin against the Lord. If we could make the journey across the waves, then we were all free. Free – and safe – and ... home?

Simeon helped me aboard, and as he took my hand

I felt a faint flush creep up my cheeks. Kata's eyes widened in surprise, which only made me blush more.

"Your vessel, my lady," said Simeon with a low bow and a broad smile. I thought I had never seen a man so beautiful.

We had parted from our Oglala companions before setting off. I had not known how to thank them.

Then Winona addressed me directly for the first time. "For you, Maggie Walton Oglala," she said, taking a string of beads from round her neck and placing them over my head. Then she produced a small pot of red dye and applied a little to each of my cheeks, her long fingers making each stroke feel like a blessing. "This is *Hunkapi* – the ceremony for the making of relatives," she explained. "One of the seven Lakota rites given to us by the Sacred White Buffalo Calf Woman. Now you are part of the Oglala forever. Part of the Great Nation and the great wind that blows freedom from coast to coast."

I did not know what to say to express my gratitude. I thought of Pearl Dimesdale, who had been adopted by the Inuit; I thought of how Madame La Barboule had made us part of her family at the emporium; I thought of the Krajeks, risking everything to help others to safety. I thought that, for all the cruelty in this word, we had encountered so much kindness, so much goodness, so much love on our journey – more than enough, surely, to defeat the hatred?

I looked at her then, really looked. And I seemed to see a halo of licking flames encircling her head, her whole form – as I had seen when she stood framed in the doorway of the derailed train. I blinked and it was gone but I was sure I had not imagined it, nor had it been a trick of the light. For a second I had seen Winona as Natty Bumppo described – as the spirit, not the skeleton; the soul, not the poor cage that trapped its mortal form.

My fingers found the beads again now as I sat in the prow of the boat pushing out into the great lake, Krajek at the helm. The moon was low on the horizon. The beads lay across my chest where Victor had once nestled. They did not fill the void but they lent it a new colour. That was the only way of describing it. A bit of warmth touched the grief in my heart and lightened it – just a little.

"What will you do with your freedom?" asked Simeon.

"I … I don't know," I stammered. My face seemed to flush whenever I looked at him. And I still wasn't sure I believed in this freedom – not yet.

"There is a settlement beyond the mountains," said the mother of the family from Georgia – Cora Douglas, she told us her name was. "Former slaves made a home there. New Heaven, they call it. More ex-slaves come to join them every year. My sister and her husband are there already, we think. We hope one day our son and our two daughters will find a way there too."

"You should join us," said one of the girls who had escaped the band of soldiers.

"Yes," said Simeon with his disarming smile. "You should. Come to Heaven with us."

I glanced at Kata, but he was staring out across the water, back the way we had come, and for some reason he would not meet my eye. "I – I don't know what we'll do. Where we will go."

In truth I think I expected every moment for our vessel to be overtaken, to hear a cry from the shore, to see a boat approaching, to hear Tom Loker's voice, see Florenzo's vengeful smile. But the journey was uneventful, the waters calm and glowing gold and coral in the sunrise. Barely an hour later, with dawn casting ruby-tipped arrows across the waves, we saw the shoreline – the shores of freedom, of Canada.

My companions were emotional. Cora Douglas was crying, as was the old grandfather from Virginia, a man named simply Thursday, who had lived seventy years a slave and could see the first dawn of freedom rising on the horizon.

The boat pulled up on to a small jetty; no need for secrecy now. There was a small crowd there to greet us – some former slaves, some white Canadians, all mingling equally. It all seemed overwhelming – impossible. A dream come true.

We clambered out – Simeon helping me, the girls laughing and dancing. Cora Douglas saw a face in the crowd that she recognised, and a voice called "Mother!" as a young woman rushed forward who had a face just like Cora's. They clung to each other, crying and crying.

I turned to Kata. His face was full of something I had not felt for so long I had almost forgotten it existed.

Hope.

I turned to take his hand. Here at last, on the shores of freedom, I could get my friend back once more. His fingers made contact with mine and for a brief second I felt a thrill of happiness, before I heard a voice that chilled me to the core.

"Maggie Walton – did you really think you could escape your fate?"

Chapter 46

We had no choice but to go with Florenzo. Whether his legal claim on Kata extended to Canada or not, whether our companions could have prevented him by force or not … all that was immaterial. For he had my father.

He told us that he had my father captive, and he threatened to kill him if we did not come.

The dream of freedom and safety had turned out to be just that – a dream. And I was just as foolish as my father for believing it might come true.

So we allowed Loker to manacle us, and Florenzo paid the slave-catcher his bounty. Kata and I were given no leave to say farewell to our boat companions, but shoved into a carriage that stood waiting for us.

How had Florenzo known we were here? Had O'Malley tipped him off? Or Ambrosz Krajek? Or William Wraithmell? Natty Bumppo? Somehow I struggled to believe any such explanation, and yet he had known we were coming. He had been waiting for us. Perhaps we would never know how. Never know who. Perhaps he had just followed his nose and smelled us out. It no longer mattered. We were his captives once more, and this time he would never let us go. It had all been for nothing. All our efforts, and those of the people who had tried to save us – all for nothing!

I was manacled so that I could not see Kata's face as we drove for hours, high, high into the mountains, through passes that grew ever narrower and ever steeper as we climbed, until, nearing sunset, with storm clouds gathering on the horizon we reached a lake smaller than that which we had crossed, and overlooked by towering snow-capped peaks. Even the beauty of this place could not dispel the despair in my soul. Eventually we reached a lonely cabin that had perhaps once been built for miners seeking gold in the hills, now forlorn and dilapidated. More like a shack than a dwelling fit for humans, a tumbledown wreck with a giant lightning rod extending from the roof, it looked out across dark waters, upon which mountains echoed in rippling reflections.

The sky was already beginning to darken as the carriage drew close, and the wind was picking up, scudding across the water in swollen eddies. I felt a shudder of premonition run through me as the horses stopped and Florenzo rudely ejected us before dismissing the coachman – and, with him, any hope of rescue. For the first time on our journey I felt like giving up. And yet I couldn't. While Kata was alive, while my father was alive, there was still hope, still a reason to keep fighting.

Then Florenzo pushed open the door to the cabin and I saw my father for the first time in nearly a month.

"Father!"

I ran to him, but he did not open his arms to greet me for he was strapped to a chair, hands bound tightly behind his back. Nor did he smile, but uttered a groan of the deepest despair. "Oh, Maggie! Maggie! Why did you come?"

He looked worse than I had ever seen him. A ghost in the shell of the man I knew – face white, dark circles rimming bloodshot eyes, hair lank, features cavernous with worry and hunger.

"Father, what have they done to you? Have they hurt you?" I flung myself at his feet, wrapping my arms round legs through which the very bones seemed to protrude.

"Oh, Maggie, my Maggie! It is I who have hurt you. I who have brought this horror upon you. Maggie, can you ever forgive me?"

"There is nothing to forgive!"

"But this is a trap, Maggie!" he cried in anguish. "I am the bait to lure you here. To your doom."

I paused, then said quietly, "I know, Father."

"You should have run!" He looked down at me with tear-filled eyes. "You should have left me, for I no longer care if I live or die, if I know you are free and happy."

"And I cannot be free or happy, knowing you are suffering." As our eyes met, so did our souls and I felt – for the first time in a long while – that I had a true father.

"Well, this is all very touching," said Florenzo. "But shall we get down to business?"

"Business?"

Florenzo had pushed Kata to the far side of the cabin where I now noticed a strange contraption stood waiting. It looked like the ancient operating table from the circus act, and suspended over it were a series of wires and tubes leading to vials of multicoloured liquids. Kata had meekly submitted to be strapped down on to the table and Florenzo was attaching wires to different parts of his body.

"Kata, no!"

Kata gave me a hopeless stare and I looked from him to my father, both bound and helpless.

I flew at Florenzo, pummelling at him with my fists. "What are you doing?" I cried. "Take us back to the circus. We'll do anything you want!"

Florenzo shoved me aside like an insect. "The circus was a mere diversion," he said, his hands busy adjusting wires, setting a gauge, tinkering with the vials of liquid. "But the time for fun and games is over. Now it is time for science – and revenge."

I was on my feet, flying at him again, trying to yank the wires out of his hand, but he pushed me harder this time and my head caught the stone surround of the fireplace, leaving me dizzied for a moment. "I – I don't understand."

I stared at the man whose face had haunted my dreams. He seemed smaller here, as if the obsession had contorted him till he was crumpled, shrunken by it.

"This creature is no sideshow, no mere circus freak," said Florenzo. "He is a miracle of science. Unlocking the secrets contained in his inhuman form will make me famous for all eternity."

"Unlocking?" My heart hammered with horrible foreboding. I struggled to my feet once more. Kata lay on the table, ashen with fear. In the sky above the cabin I heard the first crack of lightning rend the clouds. Once more I flung myself at Florenzo, but this time he spun round and pinned me against the fireplace.

"Don't you understand, Maggie Walton? I have Victor Frankenstein's journals," said Florenzo, with the same crazed look that I had seen in the ring when he was making Kata scream with pain. "And now I understand the secrets that he encoded there, which will enable me to enact the scientific miracle that will make my name live on forever."

"I don't understand!" I desperately tried to make sense of what he was saying, to recall the journals ... the scientific drawings ... the articles on the wall in his office.

"I will first extinguish the creature's life." Florenzo produced a gun and I gasped in horror. "And then I will use Victor's methods to revive the dead corpse." Another crack of lightning sounded above. "The conditions are exactly as I hoped. Everything is ready. Prepare to behold a modern miracle."

Kata had turned green and I felt as if I were going

to be sick. It was my father who uttered, "Why are you doing this?"

The storm outside was now picking up: thunder prowled around the lake, the first drops of rain hammered on the roof, and wind rattled the window panes.

For a second – just a second – Florenzo wavered, as if perhaps in the frenzy he had even forgotten himself why he was doing this.

"To make a name for myself!" he cried, waving the gun aloft. "A name greater than that of Victor Frankenstein! He created misery and destruction; I will defeat death itself. I will be a god among men. My riches and power will be unprecedented!'"

I saw another sword of lightning skim across the black waters.

"But why? For money? For power?"

"To punish Victor Frankenstein and his abhorrent fiend for the death of my sister!"

A triple fork of lightning hit the lake, fracturing it like a mirror.

"Your … sister?"

A crash of thunder followed almost immediately and Florenzo began to laugh. "You read your father's letters very carefully, did you not?"

The wind was howling like the wails of dying men.

"You know each of the monster's victims." The count cradled the gun in his hand. "Name them to me."

Florenzo's vice-like grip on my shoulder loosened just a little. My brain was working hard to process all that was happening: the sound of the wind and the thunder competing against the drumming of fear in my head; the sight of Kata strapped down, the cables attached to his body extending up to the roof of the cabin and the lightning rod I had spied as we arrived; the gun in Florenzo's hand – pearl-handled, deadly; my father bound and helpless … And all the time I was wracking my brain, trying to think of a way out of this, a way to escape, to keep Kata safe.

"Victor's brother William was the first," I stammered, my eyes running over the cables, trying to figure out a way to dislodge them before lightning struck the rod and shot thousands of volts into Kata's helpless body. For this, surely, was the culmination of Florenzo's diabolical scheme, the method Victor Frankenstein had used to harness the powers of the heavens to bring dead flesh to life.

"Then … William's nanny, Justine Moritz, who was hanged for the boy's murder," I went on, frantically searching for a solution. "Are you – are you her brother?"

"Do I look like I am related to a mere domestic servant?" said Florenzo with a curl of his lip.

A growing sense of dread flooded my heart as another crack of lightning sounded, quickly followed by another growl of thunder. The storm was coming closer. "Then … there was Henry Clerval – Victor's childhood friend. Then…"

"Yes … go on!"

My heart was thundering in my chest. My father, who had come to the truth at the same moment I had, groaned in pain.

"And Elizabeth – Victor's new bride."

A vivid flash of lightning illuminated the cabin, and a clap of thunder sounded overhead immediately after.

"Indeed. Elizabeth. The orphan girl adopted by Frankenstein's parents – daughter of an Italian nobleman named—"

"Lavenza!"

Chapter 47

Finally all the pieces of the puzzle came together. I understood the count's obsession with tracking down Frankenstein's creation; with torturing Kata and recreating the death of Elizabeth on stage; with this last gruesome experiment. I took a few steps towards him – the little boy who had never got over the loss of his big sister.

"I changed my name," he said. "A little of Frankenstein. A little of the sister stolen from me."

"But this will not bring her back!" I cried.

I recalled what La Barboule had said. Of how she had first met Florenzo searching the globe in search of a woman. I recalled the bundle of journals Mignon had seen delivered to him. Had they told of Elizabeth's death, in what manner she had died, by whose hand? How had he get hold of them? I recalled too the wall in his office. When had his obsession with punishing Frankenstein turned into an equally unholy desire to follow in his footsteps?

"She would not want this," croaked my father, his voice feeble against the sound of the storm, which rose every moment in tenor, echoing off the mountainsides around the cavernous lake, the lightning bolts coming with ever more frequency, each time closer still. "She was a creature of pure goodness. She would hate to see you torture a child!"

"*I* was a child!" cried Florenzo. "A child who lost his father to debtors' prison, who was sent to dwell with peasants in the Italian countryside. Whose sister – his only family – was taken from him by Victor Frankenstein's family!"

"Then you know what it is to be a lonely child," I said, taking another step towards him, my eyes always on the gun in his hand. "That has been Kata's fate too."

"When my father was released, our family fortune restored, he came for me. But we could not trace my sister," Florenzo went on, caught up in memories that seemed to wrack his brain so that he seemed barely aware of the cracks of lightning rending the air like claws, closer, ever closer. He seemed almost to have forgotten about Kata, about me, my father – his plan. Only his loss consumed him. And there lay our chance.

"My father died shortly thereafter, leaving me a fortune but no one to share it with. All I wanted was my sister!"

I took another step towards him. He seemed shrunken by his tale – a small boy who had lost his sister. But I could not afford to feel sorry for him.

"She is gone," I said quietly. "But this boy can still be saved."

"I don't want to save him!" Florenzo sprang away from me with a snarl, the gun now angled at Kata's head, his hand shaking and his face pale with the tremors of rage and fear and grief. "I want him punished. I want my revenge. I want to see him squirm in pain and agony as I have done. Only once he feels my pain will I be satisfied."

I saw in horror his transformation from lonely child to vengeful man. Pain had not hollowed him out as it had my father; it had turned him into a fiend. Florenzo spoke of monsters and men as if they were two separate things, and yet in him they were now one and the same.

Another crack of lightning arrived almost simultaneously with a crash of thunder, causing sparks to shoot off the cables. Kata flinched. Florenzo held the gun to the boy's temple and slowly depressed the trigger.

"What if … I can bring you … the real monster?"

It was my father who spoke.

The count turned to him, finger still tight on the trigger, eyes alight with unholy fire. "You said it was dead!"

"I saw Ishmael before we left New York," my father stammered. He had twisted himself upright on the chair so that he now faced Florenzo. "He came to see La Barboule. The *Moby Dick* had been sailing in search of the Northwest Passage. He said there had been many reported sightings of the creature."

"I – I don't believe you!" said Florenzo, his hand shaking as it held the gun.

"It's true." My father's voice was as serene as the lake we'd sailed across that morning, calm with a determination I had not seen for many a year. "Even here the people speak of him – I heard it from the driver who brought us to the cabin. They say the monster has ventured out of the ice, into the mountains."

The storm had stilled momentarily – an eerie hiatus as the lightning gathered itself for a final offensive.

"The monster … is here?"

"They say he is seeking his son."

I heard a sound from Kata and saw his eyes light up with a crazed hope.

"If I can bring you the monster, will you let Kata and Maggie go?"

I was not sure I believed my father. What he was offering was surely impossible. And yet – what if? Florenzo seemed stunned by his words, the gun forgotten. I took a step forward and as I caught my father's eye I saw he had loosed one hand from the bonds that tied him. This was our chance – our only chance! Florenzo opened his mouth to answer as the room lit up and a terrifying crack of thunder rent the air. Electricity shot through the cables, causing sparks to fly and Kata to cry out in pain.

At the same time the door smashed open and a mighty voice cried with the voice of the storm.

"Give me my son! Give me my boy!"

Chapter 48

The image I beheld recalled that which my father had described in his letters long ago. He had written of the creature of Frankenstein cradling the body of his dead creator. Now I saw the image in duplicate. A giant creature, more extraordinary than anything I had ever beheld, burst through the door, tore the bonds that held Kata prisoner and gathered his own son's body to his breast, wailing, "Forgive me, forgive me, my child!"

Kata stared up at his father, who was looking at him with an expression of such intense love it made me feel momentarily as if I were drowning. "Father," he whispered.

"Yes, my son. It is me. The cruellest of fathers, but yours nonetheless."

The boy looked up into the face of the man who had fathered him, and I knew there was no anger there, no reproach – only a desire to love and be loved. I experienced again the pang of exquisite drowning pain – for was not this Kata's true home, his true family?

Across the other side of the room my own father was staring in agony of finally-realised hope. For here was the fulfilment of his every waking fantasy; here was the colossus for whom he had sacrificed so much. He had not beheld it for nearly twenty years. The amber-flecked eyes shot with pain, the pallid skin pulled taut over the bloodless frame of the face, the raven-dark hair now shot through with grey, the magnificent stature gnarled and knotted with age, but still the same: Victor Frankenstein's magnificent creation.

"How did you know?" Kata managed to whisper.

"I heard it on the winds that carry from the southern tip to the Arctic wastes. I heard the Great Nations call to aid the boy with the rainbow soul. And I realised that it was you. That it was my son." His face crumpled in something like despair. "I thought all I was capable of creating was ugliness and pain and destruction, but too late I realised I had also made you – a thing of beauty and kindness and pure love. And I knew I must rescue my son."

"I knew you would come, Father!"

"And so did I!" yelled Florenzo in frenzied triumph, the first words he had uttered since the creature's arrival. Rain was lashing through the broken door and the wind howled through the cabin as Florenzo grabbed both my arms, pinning me to his chest. I could feel something cold against my throat – the barrel of his pearl-handled gun. "And now I have you both at my mercy!"

Kata jerked out of his father's embrace. The colossus looked up in confusion. My father froze in horror. I felt as if I were going to be sick.

"Now you too will know how it feels to lose someone you love!"

"No!" cried Kata and my father in unison.

"I will release her only if you both agree to submit yourselves to my mercy," said Florenzo. I could feel the muzzle tight against my neck; one press of his finger and it would all be over.

"No!" I said. "He will hurt you both. Kill you both! Run! Save yourselves!"

"How touching," said Florenzo, his breath hot on my neck as the wind whipped and howled around us. "And how futile! Either way I win. If you stay to save her life, I take your liberty. If you run and I kill her, then the outcome is the same, for a guilty conscience affords no freedom. You know that all too well!"

He was staring, his face alight with a hunger for revenge such as I had never seen before.

"Let her go!" cried Kata. "Do anything to me, but don't hurt Maggie."

A crash of lightning sent more sparks down the cables that had been ripped loose from Kata's body, but which lit up father and son as if in a spotlight at the emporium.

"Oh! This is better than I had hoped!" cried Florenzo. "The boy monster is in love. My work is done, for what greater pain can we endure than that of heartache!" He laughed maniacally. "And how dare a creature such as you, born out of darkness, presume to reach for such light? How can a boy created by evil and hatred believe anyone could ever love him back!"

"But I do!" I cried. "I do love him!" The words came out before I knew I had uttered them, but immediately – and unexpectedly – I knew them to be true.

And I knew also in that moment that Kata loved me too. The room seemed to stand still for a moment, but also to spin around us in giddy, creaking circles.

But then something was happening. My father had worked himself free of his bonds and had produced a second gun. He stood there on his feet, swaying, aiming it at Florenzo but not shooting, for if he did I would surely fall too.

I glanced from Kata to my father, the two people I loved most in the world. Without Florenzo, both of them would be free. Safe.

"Do it, Father!"

"No!" screamed Kata.

"No!" yelled his father, lurching for the crackling cable that ran up to the lightning rod above.

It felt as if everything happened at once. Kata lunged forward, tugging something from his pocket. His father leapt to stop him, grabbing hold of the thickest of the cables suspended from the roof as he did so. I heard a gunshot, felt a sharp pain – then there was a second shot, followed by a crack of lightning reverberating with a simultaneous roar of thunder, then the blinding light of an explosion, and I felt myself falling to the floor … and Florenzo was falling too … and there was blood and howling. I could hear my name, crying out on the winds, in a chorus of different voices.

And then darkness.

Chapter 49

The first thing I was aware of was clean sheets. Then the smell of coffee, woodsmoke and the rising sap of spring.

I opened my eyes with difficulty. Where was I? Some sort of log cabin, neatly appointed, with a freshly swept floor and red gingham curtains at the windows.

I turned my head with difficulty as my neck throbbed with a dull, low pain. I could see Kata's face in profile. He was asleep on a rocking chair beside the bed in which I lay. There was no sign of my father.

"What – what happened?"

"You're awake!"

"I don't understand. Where am I? How did I get here?"

"You were shot," said Kata, his voice gentle, his beautiful eyes filled with concern. "Florenzo tried to kill you but I— The bullet missed. It just grazed your neck, but still you lost a lot of blood. I thought… But you are awake!" He seemed so relieved, so happy. But was there more he wasn't telling me?

"My father?"

"He tried to shoot Florenzo but the gun backfired." Kata hesitated. "It caught him in the chest."

"Oh god! Is he—"

"He is alive," said Kata. "My father…"

"Yes?"

Kata's face was hard to read. He was talking to me in the soft voice one uses for small children. The voice my aunt used when she was delivering bad news. The voice of death. Of loss. Of mourning.

"I caught you when you fell and then Florenzo…" His eyes were stained with exquisite pain. "Florenzo put the gun to my head. He tried to shoot but he missed. My father had the lightning rod. He flung himself at Florenzo and…"

"And…?"

"When the lightning struck he had Florenzo in his arms. The bolt was so strong it…" His face contorted. "It killed them both in an instant."

There was a long, long pause.

"Florenzo is dead?"

"And so is my father."

Another long silence. I realised that Kata had taken my hand in his. There seemed no other way to communicate all we had to say in the silent minutes that followed.

I don't know how long it was before I asked, "How did we get here?"

Kata looked a little awkward. He reminded me for a moment of Tommy Tucker of Shadwell Basin. I had not thought of Tommy for so long, but I recalled now the expression that crossed his face when he confessed to stealing an apple or picking the pocket of a drunken mariner in the tavern.

"I carried you here," he said. "You were bleeding. I didn't know how to care for you so I carried you through the storm, across the mountains, till I found this place."

I looked at him in amazement. I had so many questions I wanted to ask but for now all that I managed was, "Where are we?"

"The settlement Simeon told us of," said Kata, his face flushing again with an expression I did not understand. "The people call it New Heaven. This cabin belongs to

Cora Douglas's sister and her husband."

I imagined the scene. The storm-wracked night. The giant boy appearing with a dying girl in his arms, soaked to the skin, asking for help. An alarming vision it must have been, and yet these people had opened their doors.

"And my father?"

"He insisted I must care for you first." Kata's face fell again. "But when I went back for him…"

"Yes?"

"He had developed a fever from his wound," Kata went on. "I carried him back through the mountains, but he has been dangerously ill."

"How is he now?" My heart was beating a furious tempo.

"Resting," said Kata. "Mrs Douglas thinks he will make a full recovery." Another long silence.

I had one more question. "You said that Florenzo missed when he tried to shoot me."

"Yes." He looked down at his large fingers entangled with my own.

"And he also missed you?"

"Yes."

"I don't understand. What made him miss … both times?"

Kata looked up a little sheepishly then reached into his pocket to produce a small wooden tube, engraved with patterns from Myanmar. The poison-dart shooter that Lae Khoe had given him.

"You shot him?"

Kata gave a bashful smile. "In the neck. Not enough to kill him, but he didn't know what he was doing."

I met Kata's smile with one of my own. "You saved my life," I said. "You saved us all!"

Chapter 50

I recovered quickly in New Heaven. Ministered to by Cora Douglas, whose gentle touch and knowledge of healing herbs reminded me of my aunt, with Kata always by my side, tending to my every need, I was soon sitting up in bed and well enough to play the games that he and I had enjoyed on the ship when it was I who had nursed him.

My father was soon up too, and besides his improved colour he seemed more at peace than I had ever known him, released at long last from the fever that had gripped him for so long.

Kata was grieving for the loss of his father, even as I rejoiced in the return of mine. He did not speak of it; he did not need to. The pain of losing a parent he had known but for a matter of minutes was something he would not soon recover from. I knew too well the dull ache of emptiness that still throbbed within when I thought of my beloved aunt, of Victor. It was a pain we would weather together over the weeks and months and years to come.

Until I was well enough to see it for myself, Kata told me about New Heaven. Lakota and Ojibwe and Mohican and many other First Peoples who had been dispossessed of their land; runaways from the slave plantations of the South; Inuit and Dene and Cree from the north driven out by the receding ice flow or the Hudson's Bay Traders; emigrants from the Old World – all fleeing persecution, starvation, despair. Outcasts – belonging nowhere and everywhere – all might find a home in New Heaven.

It was late in the afternoon when Kata carried me out on to the veranda to see the valley for myself. I was wrapped in blankets, though there was barely a chill in the early-autumn air. He carried me like a baby, as if I might break in his arms as he placed me in the creaking swing. I wondered if this is how it had been when he carried me across the mountains that night.

Kata perched beside me on the swing and I could feel the warmth of his body as we looked out across the wooded valley, bathed in the glow of late-afternoon sun. This place was beautiful. A fertile land – we would not need to cut down trees or displace other peoples to make a home. A sprinkling of houses was spread across the valley – log cabins like this one. A new community growing up out of the fresh, fertile soil.

"My father is writing to La Barboule to see if she will join us here," I said. "You could ask Mignon too – if you want."

"She wouldn't like it here," he said with a shrug. "She was born for the stage and since the circus burned down it's being run by Lae Khoe and Enano as a touring company, a collective. Everyone gets a say – and a share of the profits. Things will be much better for her now."

I said nothing, hiding the joy that leapt unbidden to my heart.

"I heard that Simeon has gone back to America." Kata was staring at the distant woods.

"Yes. Cora told me he is to be a conductor on the underground railroad," I said, keeping my voice as flat as I could manage. "So he can help other slaves escape. I think it is wonderful."

"You do?" said Kata, turning an enquiring look in my direction.

"He wasn't the settling-down type," I said. "Riding the railroad is the perfect life for him."

We sat in silence once more. Since Victor had left us, the silences sometimes stretched longer, emptier than before – I missed the way our little mouseling had run threads of understanding between us. I missed so many things about him: his bright eyes, the gentle nudge of his pink nose, the sensation of his fur beneath my fingers, his heart beating beside mine.

Now there was a new heart beating in time with my own as we gazed at the sun shimmering coral rays over the valley.

"We could belong here. We could make a new life," Kata said. "If … you want to?"

I did not reply immediately.

"Or maybe you and your father would be … safer … happier … without me?"

I looked at Kata, really looked at him – his skin bronzed from spending time in the sun-filled valley, his hair clean, and his deep-brown eyes bright with something I had not seen for so long – hope. There was grief in his expression too, and he seemed older somehow. Something had happened in the days when he had tended to me, kept me alive; the tables had turned. He had grown up. I glanced at him shyly as he sat by my side. He looked huge – I swear he had grown several inches since we arrived in Canada – his features irregular … and beautiful.

"We might be safer without you," I said, and I felt him stiffen. "But we certainly would not be happier."

He met my gaze full on and in the late-afternoon sunshine his asymmetrical features were bathed suddenly not in the colours of sunset, but in an odd halo that flickered in the myriad colours of the Northern Lights.

"You are family now," I said. "More than family."

Kata beamed then and took my hand in his. "More than family," he repeated.

"So you are staying right here," I said. "With us – with me – where you belong!"

Acknowledgements

It was 1982. *E.T.* fever swept the nation. My most prized possession was my extra-terrestrial lunch box; my favourite food was an *E.T.* biscuit which changed colour when you licked it; I wore a ra-ra skirt, maroon leg warmers and big Princess Di collars; and all I wanted was to find an alien in my cupboard with a light-up finger who needed to phone home.

My wonderful primary school teacher Mrs Cockayne decided to tune into *E.T.* fever through a class project on aliens. But instead of looking at little green men, she read us *The Iron Man* by Ted Hughes, *Stig of the Dump* by Clive King and an abridged version of Mary Shelley's *Frankenstein*. And through those stories she encouraged a group of nine year olds to think about 'otherness' – how societies and individuals treat those who are different. She asked us to consider the pain of exclusion, and the power of kindness. She showed me a different definition of 'alien', and made me see how aliens might walk amongst us – not always with long necks and fluorescent fingers, but just as in need of befriending as Spielberg's creation.

Looking back I wonder if she had an agenda. This

was, after all, the era when 'mean girls' ruled the school, their modus operandi picking on someone to exclude, to treat as a pariah – the fat kid, the thin kid, the poor kid, the kid who who hadn't watched the lasted episode of *Charlie's Angels*, who didn't know the dance moves to *Making your Mind up*. If you wanted to stay 'in' with the cool crowd then you had to join in with the persecution of the person who was 'out' – or it might be you next.

Did Mrs Cockayne read us those tales of outsiders to remind us to be kind? Did she pick stories of standing up for those who are persecuted and treated with cruelty because they don't fit in to inspire the pupils of Class J3 to our own acts of heroism? For me it was the story of the lonely 'monster' longing for human contact that stirred my imagination. I learned to be a little braver – not always as brave as I could have been – and realised that E.T. and Stig and Frankenstein's creature aren't just found in the cupboard, or on space ships, or shot through with bolts of lightning in a laboratory. And that bravery doesn't always have to be enacted on a flying bicycle.

Because of Mrs Cockayne I've always loved the spine-tingling Gothic adventure that is *Frankenstein* – I can still see the images of the monster wondering the frozen arctic wastes that she first conjured up in my mind. But she also made me see it as a story about how we treat those who are different. And about what that says about us. And in *Following Frankenstein* I have tried to write a tale about otherness, about what it means to look different, to feel different to everyone else around you. To be friendless, ostracized, abandoned – even by your own family. And to overcome that through the power of friendship, but also through the power of your own difference.

When I started writing this novel, the wonderfully wise Fox Benwell helped me to see that *Frankenstein* is also a story about disability and neurodiversity – indeed some critics see it as an early exploration of autistic spectrum conditions. Mary Shelley's wise, compassionate and philosophical original has been reinvented within popular culture so that when most people hear *Frankenstein* they think of a monster with a bolted neck, gurning and inarticulate, dangerous and disfigured. And that image has in turn become responsible for many unhelpful tropes about disability that populate literature and wider culture perpetuate. Thanks to conversations with Fox, Joanna Nadin and Moira Young on Friday morning writing sessions at BTP I considered how as writers we can challenge such unhelpful 'ableist' stereotypes and tropes – which are even embedded in the very language we use. Because, as children's authors, we have a responsibility to champion and to celebrate the 8% of children in the UK who are living with a disability. So I hope this story is one that celebrates diversity, challenges discrimination – and encourages all young readers to do the same.

Following Frankenstein – like Mary Shelley's original – also explores mental illness, family breakdown and young carers. Before the pandemic there were 800,000 young carers in the UK – one in every twelve secondary aged pupils. Post-Covid those figures have grown exponentially, as have those of children living with a parent suffering from mental illness. The average age of a young carer is thirteen, but at least 10% of young carers are under the age of ten. As a teacher I have seen the impact this has on young people – many of whom are unaware of their own quiet, unspoken heroism. So this story is in celebration and with thanks to all the young carers I've had the privilege to teach – and to the many more across the world – in recognition of the burden they carry with dignity, stoicism and love.

It's a story about families too. And the power of parental love. But most of all it's a grand adventure in the style of stories I adore – a race across America with baddies in hot pursuit. It is a mish-mash of stories I love and those I have loved teaching. From *E.T.*, *Stranger Things*, and *The Greatest Showman*, to *Moby Dick*, *Huckleberry Finn*, *Last of the Mohicans*, *The Scarlett Letter*, *Uncle Tom's Cabin*, *Hard Times* and *My Antonia*. The latter were inspired by many wonderful hours reading American Literature with my incredible A-Level students of recent years, as are the references to the Underground Railroad, Sleary's circus and the Muckrakers, with a teensy nod to *Hamilton*, Colson Whitehead, *The Mermaid and Mrs Hancock* and the inimitable Sebastian Barry (the last for my wonderful teaching partner and dear friend Steph Vernon!). Thanks to all of you guys I've woven in some of my favourite characters and journeyed across America in my imagination to all the places I longed to go to in lockdown – from the New York Bowery to the Arctic Tundra, from Shadwell Basin to the forests of Minnesota and the Great Plains, stretching endlessly west towards Manifest Destiny!

So to all the academics, literary scholars, English teachers, copy editors and well-read pedants who pick up this book I would like to offer in advance a fulsome apology. I have borrowed liberally from the great American novels and from the vast sweep of American history, peppering these pages with faces, names, places and characters with precious little regard for chronology or geography or literary anachronism. The English teacher in me offers up this defence: I *do* know that Natty Bumpo and Harvey Birch and Ishmael, Tom Loker and Antonia Krajek could not have been contemporaries; that the Underground Railroad and the Transcontinental Railway stand as anachronisms besides the son of Frankenstein; that any cartographer – ancient or modern – would dispute the routes my characters take. But this is a world inhabited by Victor Frankenstein and his creature – not our world, though very like it – in which chronology and geography and narrative run on different paths to those followed in our own. A world inhabited by literary characters whose lives intersect without undue regard for anachronism but concerned only with the simple joy of a tale well-told, a re-writing of the old bogey tale to thrill the listeners. A little like the monster itself, this story is stitched together out of fragments of other tales, brought to life with a little electricity of my own – it's not always perfect, and you can see the stitches in places, but I hope that the seventeen-year-old Mary Shelley who first created the monster would approve, and that all others will forgive my monstrous temerity.

Because I wrote a lot of this story in a coffee shop in Bath, overlooking the site where Mary Shelley penned the final manuscript of her novel. And I found myself thinking of the young woman ostracized by society, shunned by her own family for the choices she had made. And of how she turned that pain into something powerful – a cry for tolerance and kindness which has endured across the ages.

Kata and Maggie encounter lots of people who are different in this story – people who are excluded and discriminated against on the basis of race, disability, culture, gender, appearance and skin colour. We may no longer have circuses which parade people as freaks and curiosities, but social media is its own circus, and the fight for equality is far from won. Yet as a teacher, I stand in awe of this generation's ability to champion diversity, to own and celebrate their own uniqueness and that of others. So I hope young readers will see this as a story that celebrates difference, that shows how we can triumph not through excluding others, but by inclusion; not by 'fitting in' but through being authentically ourselves. Because being different can be beautiful, brave, brilliant, loving and loveable.

Oh, and since this was supposed to be acknowledgements (before I got a bit side-tracked!) I must not forget to thank those who infuse the spark of life into me and bring me alive as a writer – the amazing

Caroline Montgomery, the wise and wonderful Tom Bonnick, and the ever-patient and much-loved Jonny, Joe and Elsie.